The
RAIDERS

The RAIDERS

Garry Kilworth

mammoth

First published in Great Britain 1996 by Mammoth,
an imprint of Reed International Books Ltd,
Michelin House, 81 Fulham Road, London SW3 6RB
and Auckland, Melbourne, Singapore and Toronto

Reprinted 1997

ISBN 0 7497 2818 3

A CIP catalogue record for this book is available from the British Library

Printed and bound in Great Britain by Cox & Wyman Ltd, Reading, Berkshire

Contents

1 Town boy, country girl

Luke Tynan watched the last of the houses go by the side window and soon Stratford was behind him. He turned his head to look through the windscreen at the countryside into which his mother was driving the Ford. It was not a particularly inspiring view: a flattish, rippling landscape with a few scruffy trees and some open farmland studded with the odd house. The weather was moody and irritable, with peevish winds flicking at the hedgerows and a rumbling murkiness above.

'How old are these kids?' he asked his mother grumpily.

Beth Tynan was hunched over the wheel in that intense posture she always adopted for driving.

'Your cousins? I told you – Mary's twelve and little Billy? I think he's just past his seventh birthday.'

1

Luke's father, Jim, was normally away a lot on business. Recently, however, he had been promoted to a position in head office at Amersham in Buckinghamshire. This meant they were now searching for a new home and Luke was being sent to his aunt and uncle for the summer, to give Beth the freedom to rush off at a moment's notice to view a house.

Luke himself was thirteen. If asked to describe himself he would have said he was slim with fair, longish, curly hair parted in the middle. He believed himself to be stylish, reasonably good-looking except for a pair of sticky-out ears.

Luke didn't want to leave the streets where he had been raised. He didn't want to go to his uncle and aunt's house at Paglesham, and he was absolutely certain he was going to hate both his cousins and everything about the place on the edge of the Essex coastal marshes.

'I bet they're wimps. I bet they don't know anything about cars. I bet they can't tell a Saab from a Rover. I bet they don't know twin carbs from overhead cams. I bet . . .'

'Oh, Luke, give it a *rest*,' said his mother in a weary voice. 'I know you don't want to go, but we

2

haven't got a choice at the moment, not until our old home's sold.'

The house where he had lived all his life was on the market. The whole thing was crazy as far as Luke was concerned. Why did he have to be out of the way, when he knew he could help with the move?

Luke kept his silence after that as they sped down the dual carriageway that connected the Essex estuary with London.

By the time they came to Rochford, a market town through which they would have to pass to reach Paglesham village, Luke was thoroughly bored. Rochford looked like hicksville, and what could be beyond hicksville but a primitive nowhere-land? This thought was soon confirmed as the car sped along narrow lanes, on either side of which was absolutely nothing. The landscape was perfectly flat and stretched out on all sides like a wilderness. A great stormy sky fitted over the world like a dome, emphasising the solitude and emptiness.

Luke sat up and gasped, 'It's like another planet – you can't leave me here, Mum! Where's the houses?'

He felt as if he were in a Stephen Spielberg film.

At any moment the lightning would crack, the thunder would roll and the car engine would sputter and stop. They would be stranded out here, at the mercy of whatever lurked in those creeks he could see glinting sinisterly on the horizon.

'We'll come to the houses, don't panic,' said his mother, but she too was looking dubiously at the storm-dark bleakness around them. 'There's a nice pub on the corner of the village . . .'

'Lot of good that'll do me,' snorted Luke.

He had been told that the aunt and uncle he was going to stay with were Quakers. The only thing he knew about Quakers, from a film he had seen, was that they wore funny clothes and said 'thee' and 'thou' all the time. His uncle and aunt would probably be very serious, very boring and more than likely very strict disciplinarians.

Eventually they reached a fork in the road. Luke's mum turned right to Paglesham Eastend. They arrived at the cluster of houses on the edge of the tidal River Roach just as the sky let forth its flood and the rain came down. They both ran from the car to the second cottage and were immediately let into the living-room.

'Unusual, this,' said a plump woman in a faded

4

blue dress. 'We don't get much rain on the coastal strip – not usually.'

Luke's mum let out a false laugh. 'This is just to welcome *us*, is it?'

'Seems like it.'

Luke was then introduced to his aunt, Cynthia. His cousins were there, too: a peaky-faced small boy with a cheeky expression and a girl of Luke's age in jeans and a T-shirt. The girl had very brown eyes, almost jet-black hair, which she wore quite short with a wispy fringe, and a spray of freckles over the bridge of her nose. Luke decided she was probably quite pretty, but she had no style about her at all.

She obviously realised she was being studied because she lifted her chin a little and stared Luke directly in the eyes. She seemed to be daring him to say something. Luke decided she was not one of those girls who would take kindly to criticism: he had better watch what he said to her.

'These are your cousins, Billy and Mary, Luke,' said Aunt Cynthia. The children murmured something unintelligible and Luke murmured something equally meaningless back. Aunt Cynthia beamed at all three, as if they had just exchanged profound vows of friendship.

It seemed that Uncle Joe was still at work, out in that vast wet wilderness somewhere, doing something to the crops. Joe was a farm-worker.

The two adults went into the kitchen to make some tea, leaving Luke and his cousins in the living-room.

Luke studied his cousins without being too obvious and noted that neither of them had brand-name trainers on, or DMs, but wore some kind of canvas shoes. Mary's jeans were not Levis and her T-shirt hadn't come from Joe Bloggs. In fact, the pair of them would have been jeered off the streets of Stratford the moment they showed their faces. At the first opportunity, Luke said to Billy and Mary, 'These are Reeboks, these trainers . . .'

'Well give 'em back to him then,' said Billy, quick as a flash in a cheeky voice.

'No, I mean the brand-name.'

'So what? Anyway, you need to tie your laces,' said Mary, 'or you'll be trippin' up, won't you?'

Luke looked down at his precious Reeboks and at the street-cred way he had simply tucked the loose laces into the top holes. It was naff to tie a bow, or any kind of knot, as he informed Mary.

'Well, it looks daft to me,' she sniffed, 'and why have you got your cap on back to front?'

'To keep the sun off my neck,' snarled Luke.

Mary smiled a superior smile and looked at the rain smacking against the window.

'Where d'you think you are, Arabia?' she said sweetly.

'No – the back-end of nowhere,' retorted Luke. 'That's obvious. You don't know nothin', you two. What do you know about anything? Tom Cruise always wears his cap like this – don't you go to the movies? Haven't you even got a video?'

'We know who Tom Cruise is, even if we haven't got a video,' snapped Mary.

Luke was aghast. He looked around the living-room wildly.

'You mean you *really* haven't got a video? What about a Nintendo or Atari?'

'Not got them either,' said Billy. 'We got a telly though.'

'A Sega?'

'Nope. Just the telly.'

'Oh, great,' Luke cried. 'A telly! Big wows.'

'Don't know why you should be so sniffy,' said Mary. 'You haven't even got a *house*.'

This was true and it stopped Luke dead in his mental tracks. His cousin Mary rubbed salt in his wounds. 'Does everybody tie their shoelaces like that?'

'Yeah,' he told her.

'In that case,' she crowed, 'what's so special about it? I mean, if only certain people did it, to show they were different, then it'd be special, wouldn't it? But if *everybody* does it, why's it so cool? That's what I'd like to know.'

'It just is, that's all,' replied Luke in a quiet voice.

Uncle Joe arrived home from work, his boots covered in mud and his shirt decorated with bits of green silage. Uncle Joe wanted to know all about Luke's dad's new job and what sort of promotion he was getting.

Joe said he really didn't trust insurance salesmen, like Jim, even if he was family. Anyone who sold pieces of paper bearing dubious promises to pay somebody else a fortune if they died, or if their house fell down around their ears, or if their car collided with a lamppost, deserved to live under suspicion, so Uncle Joe proclaimed.

'Still,' said Joe, 'Jim's going to work in an office now – that's a bit different, I suppose.'

Once his mother had gone, Luke felt even more miserable. He was already homesick for his tarmac streets, brick buildings and concrete pavements. Even when the rain cleared and he was able to look out of the window, all he could see in one direction was brown fields, and in the other a wasteland of marsh reeds and muddy creeks.

'What do you *do* here?' he asked his cousin, Mary, bleakly. 'Where's the cinemas? Where's the game arcades? Do you have a youth club with snooker tables?'

'We got none of those,' said Mary, sadly. 'They sound like fun. We just got the marshes.'

Luke asked helplessly, 'Well, what do you do with 'em?'

'Billy goes fishing in the river; so does Dad sometimes, when he's not at work. I don't go 'cause you have to wait for *hours* until someone catches a fish. Or you can go conkering, in the conker season. Or just walk.'

Luke *hated* fishing and it wasn't conker season.

'I think I'll die of boredom,' he said mournfully.

His uncle and aunt were not very sympathetic when he told them how he felt about the place. Luke realised he should have guessed that, since they obviously liked living where they lived and had done so for many years.

'There's plenty to do in the countryside,' said

9

Uncle Joe, wagging his dinner knife at Luke. 'You just got to get out there and find it. Why, your aunt's doing a butterfly count for Butterfly Watch this summer. You could help her.'

Big wows, thought Luke. Counting butterflies.

'He's got good dandelions,' said Billy, with his mouth full. 'They belong to a boy called Reebok.'

'Good what?' asked Aunt Cynthia. 'Talk sense.'

'Dandelion roots – *boots*,' said Billy, looking pleased with himself. 'You know, cockney rhyming slang.'

'It's *daisy* roots and I'm not a cockney,' Luke said quietly.

'You live in London, don't you?' cried Billy.

'Yes – on the edge of.'

'Well, there you are then – cockney.'

Luke wasn't up to arguing with his younger cousin right at that moment so he let it pass. He spent the remainder of the evening in front of the television with the rest of the family until Aunt Cynthia told them they all ought to get to bed. It was around nine o'clock and still light outside.

'Up the old apples and peaches then,' said Billy, heading towards the staircase.

Luke simmered but said nothing. Instead, he followed his cousin up to their bedroom. There were three rooms upstairs, one for the adults, one for Mary, and Luke was sharing a tiny room with Billy. There was hardly enough room to squeeze between the two narrow beds.

It occurred to him, as he was undressing, that the one positive thing he had discovered was that his country relations didn't dress in black robes with lace collars and talk in old-fashioned English. Perhaps they were no longer Quakers? Maybe they had left the Society of Friends, as Luke's mum said it was officially called? He crawled into bed and immediately fell asleep.

The next morning he was awoken by a strange sound, like someone being strangled. His eyes wide open, Luke listened for it again. It was a couple of minutes before he realised what he was hearing was a cock crowing in the backyard. He could hear the chickens clucking too, a dog barking somewhere, pigeons cooing, seagulls carking, and a whole cacophony of country noises.

He sat up in bed and stared at the window, remembering how miserable he was in this primitive place.

However, the sun was shining comfortingly through the gap in the curtains and Luke could hear bacon sizzling in the pan downstairs. The

11

pleasant smell of the frying bacon wafted up through the cracks in the floorboards and flowed in slow meandering rivers through the gap under the door.

From the yard outside came other odours, but not unpleasant: warm chicken-feather and dog's-coat smells, mingled with the faint aroma of field dung and baked earth. It produced within Luke an old-fashioned feeling, a sense of well-being.

Billy was still fast asleep, the little hump in the next bed rising and falling slowly to soft breathing. It did not seem so bad now a new day had come, though Luke was absolutely sure he was going to be bored stiff by nine o'clock. He went to the window, pulled the curtains back and stared out over the creeks.

The tide was out and the river, just a hundred metres away, had only a sliver of silver running between two wide muddy banks. In the creeks that surrounded the river there was no water at all: just a grey-brown mud which shone where the sun struck it. Boats lay on their sides, waiting for the water to return, their rigging clattering against wooden and aluminium masts. Old, rotten hulks lay in the mud, here and there, abandoned to a sinking fate. Clus-tered around darker patches on the sludge were bunches of unknown birds busily sticking their beaks in and out of the mire.

Billy stirred and threw back his bed covers.

'I dreamed I was in China,' said Billy. 'They don't half talk funny there. Couldn't understand a word. I was speakin' it, but I didn't know what I was saying myself.'

Luke turned and stared at his cousin. 'I've got lots of Chinese friends,' he said. 'They talk English.'

'Well these ones didn't – they talked China language – you want to hear some?'

'No,' said Luke coldly, not willing to put up with Billy's nonsense this early in the morning. 'I want to get washed and dressed.'

A ginger cat suddenly appeared from nowhere and clung with its forepaw claws to the outside of the sash-cord window frame. The window slid down with a crash. Having forced an entry, the cat leaped into the bedroom, on to Luke's bed. The animal eyed him suspiciously while Luke pulled on his trainers. The whole episode scared the daylights out of Luke.

'Who's that?' he asked Billy.

'Cat burglar,' answered his cousin. 'Twiddles. Next door's. We haven't got a cat, but Twiddles comes in to steal some grub when he feels like it. He probably smelled the bacon frying – if he gets any, it's yours he's got, all right?'

Luke threw his pillow at Billy, then finished dressing, before descending the stairs to the kitchen below. Twiddles followed him down. As the pair entered the kitchen, his aunt turned to him and clucked in disapproval.

'Luke, you shouldn't bring next-door's cat in with you – Twiddles steals things from the breakfast table.'

'I-I didn't,' muttered Luke, indignantly.

Mary came into the kitchen. 'Oh, no,' she said, 'Luke's let Twiddles in.'

Billy followed Mary saying, 'I told Luke not to, but he wouldn't listen.'

'I-didn't-bring-him,' said Luke, evenly. 'He came on his own, you know that, Billy.'

Mary tutted and shook her head. 'Just wait until Dad comes down – then there'll be fireworks, Luke. Dad hates cats in the kitchen, especially cats like Twiddles. I wouldn't like to be in your shoes . . .'

2 Raiders from the sea

Luke stood there in stunned and indignant silence, not knowing how to defend himself.

Of course, they had been teasing him. Luke's uncle wasn't even in the house, having left already for work. Luke was a bit peeved with them all.

'That wasn't fair,' he said, as he stared at Twiddles gobbling down some bacon fat he had been given. 'You were making fun of me.'

Mary smiled at him warmly. 'You're tough. You can take it.'

Aunt Cynthia ruffled his hair. 'It was just a little joke – sorry if it upset you, Luke. It just seemed to slip into place. Twiddles always has his breakfast here.'

Luke's feathers were eventually smoothed down as he realised he was being a bit churlish. 'Well, all right then,' he said, sitting down at the table.

He ate some cornflakes but when he tried to eat his boiled egg, he found he couldn't finish it.

'Feeling a bit Fred and Nick today, are we?' said Billy cheekily. 'Not eatin' our egg?'

Luke stared down at his half-eaten egg and realised what Billy was talking about.

'It's Tom and Dick – *sick*,' he said. 'Billy, if you can't get the rhyming slang right, stop using it.'

After breakfast, Luke lounged around the house for a while. Aunt Cynthia had gone to her part-time job at the boat-yard where she sold fibreglass dinghies to yacht owners, fishermen and anyone else who wanted to paddle about on the river. She had, as usual, taken Billy with her. Luke was left wondering whether he was allowed to switch on the television or not when Mary suggested they go out to the salt marshes beyond the two parts of the village.

'What's to see?' he asked her. 'Any stock-car racing around here? Any drag cars?'

'Cars? No, nothing like that. We could go and watch the twitchers,' said Mary. 'Sometimes they get thirsty and send you to the shop for an orange juice or something. You can earn money like that.'

'You mean run errands?'

Mary nodded enthusiastically, her short black curls bobbing on her head. 'That's it.'

Something was puzzling Luke. 'What's a *twitcher*?' he asked tentatively, not knowing whether he was going to be ridiculed for his ignorance. In Stratford, if you didn't know something you ought to know, you were jeered out of sight.

Mary was not into scoring points the way the kids were on the streets of Stratford; she replied to his question as if it were the most natural thing in the world to be polite to a fellow human being who was out of his normal environment.

'Why, it's a *bird-watcher*. The salt marshes are full of different kinds of birds and we get twitchers from all over. You can recognise them by their clothes – they wear these drab green and brown things – and carry big binoculars or telescopes on tripods. And cameras too! They come in all shapes and sizes, do twitchers, mostly men, but some women too.'

'Twitchers!' laughed Luke. 'That's a good nickname.'

'It's what they call themselves,' said Mary. 'It's not meant to be derogatory.'

Derogatory, thought Luke. There was more to Mary than met the eye. Having shown his

17

ignorance once, he didn't ask her what the word meant, though he had a good idea. It was one of those words that teachers used when they wanted to be nasty in a superior way. '*You* are an asinine individual, Tynan, and unworthy of an education.' That kind of nasty.

'All right then,' he said. 'Let's go and look for twitchers.'

Mary left a note for her mother saying she was taking Luke out on to the marshes. Then they were out of the house, using a dirt track to lead them down to the river. Once they reached the earthen dyke, which kept the land round Paglesham from becoming flooded at high tide, they climbed to the top of it.

The dyke was around four metres high, covered in a thick, coarse grass. Once on the crest, Luke could see for miles, there being no obstacles on the flat landscape. To the north, Mary told him, was Wallasea Island, Clements Marsh and Paglesham Creek, and to the south, Barling Marsh. Across the river, which was now full of water, was Potton Island. She suggested they walk northwards along the dyke, to Paglesham Creek.

There was the smell of salty plants in the air, enriched with the pong of mud and rotting shellfish.

Luke was unused to such an odour outside a fish market and it took a bit of getting used to. It was a fine day though, the sun sparkling on the water. The tide was on the flow now and the boats – yachts, skiffs, cocklers, dinghies – going up and down the river and creeks made an interesting spectacle. There were also one or two fishermen using their casting-rods from the bank, or out in rowing-boats.

Round the river the marsh reeds formed a soft-looking sea of green-brown, moth-eaten where a creek reached deep inside.

'What's that place over there?' said Luke, pointing to a village to the west.

'That's Canewdon,' replied Mary. 'You know, King Canute? It's where he made his camp when he fought with Edmund Ironside, the English king. King Canute came up the river with his Viking longboats and crushed the English army. It was called the Battle of Assundun. Afterwards his men said Canute could do anything. To prove it they said he could stop the tide coming in and make the waves go back. Of course, he couldn't.'

'I only asked,' said Luke, a little peeved, not expecting a lecture on British history.

The dyke itself was studded with concrete pill-boxes left over from the Second World War. As they passed one of these, a group of boys and girls emerged. One of the boys, about Luke's age, glared at the pair.

'Who's that, Mary Jackson?' the boy nodded at Luke. 'Where d'you dredge him up from?'

Luke bunched his fists, expecting trouble, but Mary said, 'If you must know, Johnny Elms, he's my cousin, Luke.'

Johnny Elms continued to glare at Luke, who wanted to say something like, what are you lookin' at, moon-face? but was too unsure of himself in his present situation to do anything more than glare back. Eventually he felt Mary tug at his T-shirt and he followed her away from the group.

'That your boyfriend?' he asked Mary when they were out of earshot.

'Used to be,' said Mary, 'last year.'

That was all he managed to get out of her on the subject.

They reached Paglesham Creek, which was really an expanse of several creeks, within the hour. There they found the bird-watchers lying on the land side of the dyke, their cameras and binoculars pointed out over the creeks. In their camouflaged outfits they looked as if they were an army patrol attacking something out on the river.

'Do you know the names of all the birds?' Luke asked Mary.

'Well,' she replied, enigmatically, 'I know most of the cranes and rails, and shanks and godwits, but there are so many sandpipers and it's hard to tell the difference . . .'

'Sorry I asked,' he said, impressed but trying not to show it.

'We'd better not just go walking through, or we'll scare some of the birds,' whispered Mary. 'I'll just show you a few of the paths through the marshes, then you can come here yourself when you like . . .'

Some of the paths she revealed to him were not obvious, being hidden in the sea poa grass. Secret and cryptic ways had always appealed to his sense of drama and he imagined himself foiling a drug-smuggling gang here. He could see, to his delight, that there was danger about, with mud slicks deeper than the height of a man, and flash floodtides that swept in around the bends of the river at torrential pace.

None of the twitchers asked them to run errands, but still, Luke enjoyed the afternoon. When Mary said it was time to go home Luke told her he would rather stay on for a bit.

'Well,' she said, looking at her watch, 'it's nearly five o'clock. They'll be worried if we don't get back soon.'

'I'll stay just another hour,' said Luke. 'You tell your mum I won't be long.'

Mary went off along the dyke. By now most of the twitchers were packing away their equipment and setting off for home. The tide was out now and the muddy creeks were exposed to the late afternoon sun. Luke followed a winding path through the crazed creeks, finding fresh inlets and watercourses through the marsh. There was no playground like this in Stratford. If you wanted wilderness there, you went and played around the garages owned by residents of the high-rise blocks, or under the railway-bridge arches.

A magical monster sun dipped lower in the sky becoming larger and redder, slanting its rays in across the river. The reeds looked as if they were on fire, adding to the mysterious atmosphere of the marshes at twilight. The sounds of the birds had ceased, giving way to noisy insects and frogs. Dragonflies like sapphire darts zipped over the water, hovered still as death, then zipped away again into the gloaming.

Suddenly Luke came across a creek where a huge hull was half-buried in the mud. It was a long, lean boat with a high, curved prow. There was some kind of yawning bird's head carved on the top of the prow, but he couldn't tell what it was exactly because the mud still covered it. Luke studied the hulk with mounting interest.

A seagull landed on the prow, stared in Luke's direction and then let out a loud and startling *cark*! as if trying to draw Luke's attention to the wreck.

The boat was nothing like any craft he had seen on the river that day. There, in the glow of the dying evening, it appeared like some fairytale ship. He could see no evidence of a deck, but there was a set of raised cross planks with a hole where a mast might go. A single mast. There were no markings visible of course, for the whole hulk was covered in grey and black mud.

There was something about the craft which made Luke decide it was quite ancient. Then, with a tingle of excitement, Luke remembered what Mary had said about King Canute. That looks like a Viking ship, he told himself in some disbelief. It's the right shape.

A Viking ship! Well, hadn't Canute come sailing up the river with his longboats? Surely though, Luke thought, a wooden boat wouldn't have lasted so long. He wasn't *exactly* sure when King Canute had invaded England, but he knew from his lessons that the Vikings had been around in AD 900. That was a thousand years ago. Could the wood have lasted a thousand years?

He paced it out, along the dyke, and found the hulk was approximately twenty-two metres long.

After staring at the wreck for a long time and becoming more and more convinced that it was a Viking ship, Luke realised he ought to be getting back to the cottage. He began jogging to the dyke, while behind him the sky suddenly clouded over, bringing an early darkness from the east. When he reached the dyke, Luke turned and looked back into the quickening twilight.

His heart gave a jump as he saw a figure standing there, near to where the Viking ship lay.

Due to the dim light the figure was vague and insubstantial, mingling with the dark background clouds. Luke peered into the deepening dusk, trying to make out some details. It seemed to be a long-bearded man, standing tall and sturdy, with a conical helmet on his head. The man raised his right arm in a kind of salutation, clearly inviting a return gesture from Luke. Luke waved tentatively, and then the figure melted into the gloaming, lost in the fading scenery as the evening swept in over the reeds and hid the marshes from the eyes of humankind.

Once the shape had evaporated into the dusk, Luke was not sure he had seen anything at all. Perhaps it had been the tangled mists rising from the marshes to form the shape of a man? Or wisps of cloud blown in from the edge of the river, distorted into an image? Whatever it was, the vision was there and gone within a few moments.

Luke broke out into a full run along the top of the dyke, the light from the west still strong enough for him to see his path. He hoped not to upset his aunt by his lateness. However, when he eventually arrived back at the cottage, he found his uncle already home and the family waiting anxiously for his return. He tried to apologise but ended up stumbling over his words. Joe was not pleased with him.

'Is this how we're going on?' said Joe. 'Are you going to be a worry to us?'

'No, I said I'm sorry, Uncle. I just – I just lost track of the time. I was watching the boats on the river and I just lost track.'

Joe sighed and looked at Cynthia. 'Well, I know how it is myself sometimes, walking home from work. The river drifts along so lazy and slow – like some giant snake swimming through the marshes – the day soon disappears down its throat.' He wagged a gnarled and soil-engrained finger in Luke's face. 'But just you mind your aunt – don't give her no more worry, you hear? She's got enough to concern her without having to fret over kids lost on the marshes.'

His uncle left it at that.

Once they were sitting down to the re-heated dinner, Billy said to Luke, 'Been having a baker's at the marshes, eh?'

'Bakers?' repeated Luke, having no idea what Billy was talking about. 'What do you mean?'

'You know baker's hook – *look*.'

Luke sighed. 'You mean *butcher's*. Bakers don't use hooks, do they?'

'Yes they do,' replied Billy with some dignity. 'They use a hook to pull out the trays of bread after they've been baked in the oven. I think you've got it wrong, Luke – I think it's a baker's hook . . .'

'Uncle,' said Luke, ignoring Billy, 'you know what I saw on the marshes today?' There was suppressed excitement in his voice which caught the attention of the whole table. Everyone paused in their attempts to penetrate the steak and kidney pie crust – Cynthia was not a good cook, since she was more interested in her part-time work – and listened.

'What did you see?' asked Joe. 'The twitchers twitching?' He grinned, as if he'd made a joke, then went back to chipping away at the concrete crust.

'A Viking ship!' exclaimed Luke. 'I'm sure it was. It was half-buried in the mud, but it was the right shape.'

Joe looked at him and blinked. 'Oh, I don't think so,' he said.

'Yes, yes!' cried Luke. 'I might be a town boy but I go to school, same as everyone else. I've seen pictures of Viking ships. I know what they look like.'

Joe shook his head. 'Probably some old fishing smack. You get a lot of hulks out there in the creeks. How big would you say it was?'

'I paced it out – I know the length of my stride, Uncle. It was about twenty-two metres long.'

A forkful of cabbage was on its way up to Joe's mouth and it stopped halfway.

Joe stared at Luke. 'How long you say?'

'Just about twenty-two metres, Uncle, I'm sure it

was. And I'd guess about five metres wide. That's got to be a Viking longboat hasn't it? I mean, how long's a fishing smack?'

Luke waited in painful suspense for his uncle's answer.

'Well,' said Joe at last, 'not twenty-two metres – not any that come up this river, anyways. But I still think you must have got it wrong. That there mud preserves stuff a long time, but why, it's been near on a thousand years – maybe more.'

'Yes, but it would be important if it was, wouldn't it?' said Mary. 'I saw a programme on telly about some Saxon gold torques that were found in Suffolk. They were ever so valuable.'

'Gold is, isn't it?' cried Billy. 'This boat wasn't made of gold, was it Luke?'

'No, not gold. But Uncle, maybe the mud *did* stop it rotting away. You've got to come and look.'

'I haven't got time to go traipsing over the marshes looking for boats. I've got to go to work, young man. You don't get your food on the table by taking days off to stroll around the countryside.'

'But I could meet you from work. Mary could come with me to show me the way. We could take you to where the hulk is. It wouldn't take all that long, would it? Please, Uncle.'

'I don't know. You only got here yesterday,' grumbled Joe. 'There's been people around here ever since Adam and Eve and they've not seen any Viking ships. What makes you think you've got any better eyes than they have?'

This aspect of things did worry Luke, but he guessed that any twitchers or anglers who had seen the boat had not guessed its origin. They were surely single-mindedly concerned with locating wading birds and fish. It was only because Mary had been talking to him about King Canute that he recognised the ship for what it was. Luke's grand-mother had often said that it took new eyes to see through to old truth.

'*Please*, Uncle Joe – please!'

Luke deliberately didn't say anything about the vague figure, knowing it would not help his cause.

'Oh, give the boy an hour, Joe,' said Cynthia. 'He's had a rough time of it, what with being tem-porary homeless and all. Let him show you the boat.'

Joe looked at Cynthia and then nodded slowly.

'All right then – tomorrow evening, on the way home from work, but I'll bet it's just a wild-goose chase . . .'

That night, before going to sleep, Luke thought

about the figure on the marshes. Had he really witnessed it? Or had the twilight world with the strange light-and-dark sky, the quietness of the marshland, as day gave way to evening, and the bleak, empty landscape been so atmospheric as to produce images in his brain?

Just got the spooks, he told himself. Bound to in a place like that, all wide open and no noise.

But even as he fell asleep he realised he didn't believe himself.

3 The birdland man

The following evening Luke and Mary went to the farm where Joe worked and met him in the barn. From there the three of them took a track across the low-lying fields to the dyke. When they reached the creek where Luke had seen the wreck, there was nothing to be seen. Luke stared down at the bare mud in anguish, wondering if he had got the right place.

'It was here, Uncle – I'm sure it was.'

Joe shook his head. 'Maybe you made a mistake, Luke?'

'No, I saw it *here*.' He looked around wildly, studying the other creeks nearby. Surely it had been *this* creek? Yet they all had similarities. In fact, they varied only in the shape of the basin scoured out by the river. Luke tried to get his bearings on something other than the shape, which he had not noted in particular. His eyes alighted on a plant he had seen the previous evening.

'What's that mauvey stuff there, Mary?' he asked.

'That's sea lavender, Luke, but it grows everywhere in the salt marshes.'

'And that?' he cried, pointing to another plant.

'Bladderwort,' she replied.

Joe said, 'You won't get nowhere with looking at plants, Luke. They grows all over.'

Luke saw that his uncle and cousin knew what they were talking about and he felt crushed inside. He *had* seen the Viking ship's wreck though, and it was around here somewhere. Now he was not so certain he had the right creek, but he would come out again tomorrow and look until he found it. It was the only thing he could think of doing.

Joe stared at Luke and could see he was disappointed. 'I'm sorry, lad,' he said. 'They're very confusing, these marshes – to us, let alone a boy from London. You can't be expected to find your way through 'em after only a day.'

'Well,' Luke said, 'I'll look for it some more tomorrow – we've got to get home now I suppose?'

'Mum will be waiting with the dinner,' Mary said.

'And we know what a warmed-up dinner's like, don't we?' Joe murmured.

So the three of them took the snaking route along the dyke to Paglesham Eastend without finding the hulk.

Over the next few days Luke searched the creeks without success, becoming more upset all the time because of his failure to relocate the wreck. On some days Mary helped him look. She said she believed Luke *had* seen something and this meant a lot to the boy from the city.

Billy proved to be a chatterbox and was relentless in his efforts to misuse cockney rhyming slang, but Luke found that tolerance was the only answer. You could not suppress Billy with complaints, or even threats.

Ten days after Luke had arrived at Paglesham, his dad drove down from London to see if he was all right. On a walk down to the dyke, Luke hopefully asked his dad if he was likely to buy a new house soon.

'Doing my best, old son. Your mum's out looking right now. Can't move any faster than we're going at the moment. Anyway, you know, you'll still have to leave all your old pals behind. Amersham isn't Stratford.'

'It's not fair. I don't want to move away from my friends.'

'I know it's hard, but we haven't got a choice. At least I'll be home all the time now. We'll be a proper family. I can't commute from Stratford to Amersham every day – you'll make new friends, you'll see.'

'It's not easy at my age. You get jeered at being new.'

Luke's dad sighed, knowing that anything he said was not going to make things right for Luke.

The walk was finished in silence and Luke's dad went back to London leaving Luke utterly miserable. Amersham was an unknown country, and Luke was going there without any maps in his head.

No one in Amersham would know whether Luke was good or bad at anything. Any achievements, any victories, on the sports field, or in the classroom, or out in the Stratford streets, would be unknown. Luke would have to make his mark all over again. It was like starting life from zero, except that he wasn't a baby any more.

'It's not fair,' he said to Mary. 'People won't want to know me. They won't know what I can do, and I can't tell them or it would sound like bragging.'

'They soon get over that. It sounds horrible, but you could be one of those silent types – sort of *mystery* man, you know? Then they would think you'd done great things but were too modest to talk about your achievements.' She paused, then added, 'It doesn't worry me that people don't know what I can do. I would worry that they didn't know how I *felt* – I would want them to know how I feel about things.'

'That's because you're a girl. Girls worry about things like that. Boys worry about people taking them seriously.'

Luke rose very early the next morning to catch the ebbtide. It was a cool, slightly overcast day, with a sharp wind blowing in from the east. Luke had been told that winters on the marshes were desperately cold, with gales overspilling the North Sea and sweeping across the flatlands. He believed it. Even now, in midsummer, it was chilly once a wind sprang up and began tangling the tall reeds and grasses of the marshland.

On the river the last yachts were limping home at acute angles, anxious to reach mooring buoys before the dregs of the river drained out of the estuary into the sea. Soon they would settle on to the mud, those with double keels or keelless bottoms remaining upright, others falling tamely on to their sides. A forest of masts and booms would litter the skyline.

Johnny Elms was standing on the second pillbox, reeling in a line.

'Wuppa, Necktie,' he said in the local greeting, though without a trace of friendliness.

'Wuppa yourself, Oaktree,' replied Luke, falling in immediately with the insulting twisting of surnames.

'When you going back to London then, city slicker?'

Luke was inclined not to answer the brusque question at first, then decided against silence.

'End of summer, I suppose. What's it to you, local yokel?'

'Sooner the better,' answered Johnny Elms.

'No arguments there,' said Luke, 'with blokes like you around.'

And the pair of them left it at that.

Luke spent the day scouring the marshes for his precious Viking craft, upsetting a few of the twitchers with his rummaging through the reeds. When evening came he was no nearer to discovering which creek held the secret, and he started to walk back along the dyke towards the cluster of houses in the south. At one point, where the dyke looped, Luke took a short cut across a reedy patch of ground – and tripped over a body.

Luke went sprawling on his hands and knees. He immediately jumped to his feet, however, and stared back at the figure on the ground. It was a man. Perhaps a *dead* man, since there was no movement. The person's face looked pale and drawn. Perhaps he had drowned and had been washed up in one of the creeks? A horrible, chilling feeling ran through Luke, making his face tingle. Finally, after a good two or three minutes, to Luke's relief the man moved and sat up. He wasn't dead after all.

'I'm – I'm sorry,' Luke said. 'I didn't see you there. Are you a twi . . . a bird-watcher?'

The man did not have the usual pieces of equipment on him, nor was he dressed like a twitcher. He had on a grey T-shirt, ragged jeans and old black plimsolls. His hair was cropped short. Set in his lean face were two of the darkest eyes Luke had ever seen. The man stood up and Luke saw that he was very tall – at least a head taller than Joe, who was not short – and he had a kind of vacancy about him. His teeth seemed to be bunched in the front of his mouth, giving him a hollow-cheeked appearance. A shock of badly cut hair stood up from his scalp, the colour of dead reeds. While Luke spoke to him the man kept his face averted, as if he was afraid of looking at the person speaking to him.

Luke said 'Sorry!' again, scrambled up the dyke and was on his way once more.

When Luke felt confident enough to look back, the man was standing on the top of the dyke, his long thin arms dangling by his sides, staring out over the river towards Potton Island.

That evening, at dinner, Luke mentioned the encounter to his aunt and uncle, and asked if they knew the man.

'That'll be Tam,' said Cynthia. 'Tam Goodson. He's a strange one, that one – but he'll do you no harm.'

'Why wouldn't he speak to me?' asked Luke.

'Shy,' answered Cynthia. 'Dreadfully shy. He's a dengie, you see. Brought up in a wreck on the marshes by his dad. He won't speak to no one, not Tam . . .'

''Cept himself,' said Joe. 'Talks to himself all the time, does Tam. Man's a simpleton. Empty-headed. Doesn't even know what time of day it is.'

'It's such a shame,' said Cynthia. 'Nice lad, too.'

After dinner Luke and Mary went out into the back garden to sit on the seat Joe had made with a plank and two barrels, to watch the sun go down into the plain of reeds.

'What's a dengie?' asked Luke. He pronounced it 'denjee' as his aunt had done.

'The Dengies is the real name for the salt marshes – that's what they're called on the map. We call people who live in the marshes dengies – it's our name for marsh hermits. My dad says during the war they gave rifles to the dengie men, in case the Germans invaded and, afterwards, the government couldn't get them back. Some of the dengies still have their guns and use them to shoot wild geese when they visit in the winter – we get thousands of brent-geese from Lapland and places north.'

'He doesn't look that old, this Tam.'

'No, *he's* not from the war – his dad was. Like Mum says, Tam was brought up by his dad in an old wreck out deep in the marshes, deeper than I've taken you, and he still lives there – Tam, that is. His dad's dead now. Tam's ever so shy, like Mum says, and doesn't speak to people at all. He knows everything about the marshes, though. Every flower, every bird – everything. You see him sitting in Rochford Library and it's always a bird book or a book on marsh plants. I think he would be quite clever if people let him be.'

'How come he can read and write if he was brought up on the marshes?

Mary said in a maddeningly superior voice, 'You shouldn't make assumptions just because his dad was a dengie. Once upon a time his dad was ordinary, but then something happened and he went to live in the marshes. I think his wife run off or something. Anyway, he taught Tam to read and write – and lots of other things too, I expect.'

Luke felt suitably chastised for assuming wrongly.

The pair of them watched a big red sun sink slowly into the marshes, as if it were being sucked down by the mud. The garden songbirds gave way to the crickets and the frogs, the two separate choirs – one of the day, the other of the night – changing places without any fuss. Gnats came out in swarms, filling pockets of air chosen for reasons completely unfathomable to human understanding. Martins and swifts swooped on these knots of gnats, gathering their suppers. Soon there was nothing to be seen but pin-pricks of light out in the blackness.

Two days after Luke's first encounter with Tam he ran into him again. Tam was staring at a notice pinned to a fence post on the edge of the marsh. Tam looked distressed and kept shaking his head. Luke went over and read the notice, which was an official document.

NOTICE OF PROPOSED DEVELOPMENT

Sintra Marina Developers Ltd hereby give notice of a development to take place on the area known as 'The Dengies' between Paglesham Churchend and the River Crouch south to north and Paglesham Creek and the River Roach west to east. Drainage of the area will begin on the date specified below.

The date was only a short time away.

'What's it mean?' said Luke, more to himself than anyone else.

'It means they's going to kill all the birds and frogs, the newts and fish, an' the dragonflies – everything – they's going to kill everything on this here marsh.'

Luke stared up in astonishment at Tam, whose normal shyness had been driven away for a few moments.

'You spoke to me. They said you don't speak to anyone.'

'It's the marsh. They's going to take my home an' all away, and leave no place for the birds.'

Luke thought about this for a few minutes. Marinas had been built at home around the dockland areas of the Thames and he rather liked them – they usually had cinema complexes on them. But Tam was right: if the developers moved in they would turn the whole area into a concrete marina, which would be useful and pretty enough in its way, but it would leave no place for any wildlife. Luke had helped his mother and a protest group save a Stratford guildhall building from destruction and knew that was how to fight the developers.

'We'll have to fight 'em, Tam – that's what we'll have to do,' he said in a determined voice.

Tam turned slowly and stared down at Luke.

'That's what Svyen said to me, when we first see this notice. I'll go and get my daddy's gun then.'

4 Raiders from the land

Tam ran away, out into the marshes.

Luke, appalled by what he had heard Tam say, followed after him.

'Tam, you mustn't use a gun. That's not what I meant. If you use a gun the police will come and put you in jail . . .'

The tall man refused to stop. Luke tried to keep up with him, watching where Tam put his feet in order to keep on firm ground. Once, a flock of wading birds flew up out of the reeds, startling Luke. Still he kept after Tam, determined not to let him get too far ahead. Inevitably, Luke finally slipped into the bog and immediately sank to his hips in deep ooze.

'Help! I've fallen in!'

Luke could feel the mire sucking him down. He thrashed around, trying to reach a clump of grass to pull himself to safety. Such was his fear he did reach his goal. However, once the grass was in his hand, it tore away from the bank, leaving Luke still sinking. A godwit landed maddeningly near; made safe by its lesser weight and size, it walked across the surface of the very mud which had trapped Luke.

Just when Luke was giving way to a kind of horrified acceptance of his fate, his feet touched something hard. He had reached the solid ground beneath the morass. Ugly though his situation was, he was not going to suffocate in mud. He pulled his arms clear of the slime with horrible slucking sounds, but that was as far as he could get. The rest of him was well and truly held by the cold, firm grip of river silt that had been gathering for millennia.

'Somebody help me!' yelled Luke. 'I can't get out!'

A curlew sandpiper answered him with its own plaintive cry, as if it too was lost on some distant reach.

Suddenly, a new danger began to creep into the creek – the tide had turned. Water was sliding across the surface of the mud, gently smoothing out the wrinkles in its wake. It trickled around the island knobs of poa grass, along narrow channels cut by its parent earlier, over whaleback humps, through the gigantic ribs of old wrecks, into the little basin where Luke was struggling helplessly.

'I'm going to drown,' Luke whispered to himself.

Before very long the oncoming trickle would become a steady rush of water, twisting and swirling savagely through the winding maze of creeks, until it reached the place where Luke was held captive. It would not take long to fill the bowl of mud until the brackish water reached the waiting samphire plants round the lip. The mudworld would become a waterworld and Luke would lie beneath its surface. He yelled again, long and loud, his voice full of the terror of his predicament.

'HELP!'

Suddenly, he felt a hand on his collar. He was gradually hauled from his near grave, the mud trying to cling on to him all the way, not wishing to let its victim go. Then, with another of those slucking sounds, he was finally free. He found himself, covered in black stinking ooze, lying on firm ground and looking up at a man carrying a rusted bolt-action rifle.

'Tha-thank you, Tam,' gasped Luke, fighting for his breath, waiting for the shock to leave him. 'Thank you.'

Without a word, Tam picked him up and carried him back along the path. It led to another creek in which an old Thames barge, still bearing fragments of its reddish-brown sail clinging to its booms, was buried to its gunwales in mud. Tarred planks of wood had been nailed round the lip of the craft, presumably to stop high water from entering. A gangplank joined the listing deck to firm ground. It bent dangerously under the weight of the two bodies.

Luke was deposited on a sun-bleached, salt-worn deck, whose planks were warped and split, rusty nails poking up like little soldiers. There were rotten coils of rope, weathered old boxes and drift-wood, iron anchors, chains, and other seashore paraphernalia scattered fore and aft.

A kind of cabin had been fashioned amidships of marine ply, which had also twisted out of shape as it had not been varnished for at least a score of years. A hurricane-lamp, on which the sun spark-led, swung from the boom. The whole beached craft carried the odour of brine, shellfish – the shells of which were in evidence everywhere, cockles, whelks, winkles and mussels – and estuary ooze.

At first Tam stuttered something unintelligible. Luke deliberately looked away from him, in order not to embarrass him. Finally Tam managed to conquer his shyness and, blushing, got out two understandable words.

'M-m-m-my – house.'

Then he busied himself with coiling an old rope that had already been perfectly coiled.

'Er, very nice,' replied Luke. 'Look, can I strip off and wash myself? Have you got some clean water?'

Tam, still stuttering a little, told Luke there was a rain-barrel with fresh water down below, though he always washed in the river water. Luke said river water would be fine.

He stripped down to his underpants and went to a tank in the bows pointed out by Tam. There he washed away the smelly mud from his body. Then he rinsed his clothes through and hung them on one of the many lines that criss-crossed the craft from broken mast to various stanchions.

As he dried himself in the warm wind, Luke studied his host. He wondered what it would be like to *be* such a man. Did he use real soap to wash with or did he make his own out of animal or vegetable fats, the way Luke had seen it done in a TV programme about the Middle Ages? How did he clean his teeth? Where did he get his clothes from? What did he do all day?

'How do you clean your teeth?' Luke heard himself asking.

'With a twig,' replied Tam, unabashed. 'A – a twig with its end m-m-mashed.'

Tan sat fiddling with the rifle. Luke read the words on the breech of the weapon: *Lee Enfield Mk 4*. The gun did not look in very good condition.

'Does that thing work?' he asked Tam eventually.

Tam looked miserable. 'Not much, it don't. It don't shoot no more. B-but it scares people.'

Luke felt as if he were the grown-up and Tam was the child.

'You can't go around shooting people – or even scaring them. They'll put you in prison for that.'

Tam's face set itself and he stood up, tall and straight. 'I got to save the birds,' he said, firmly. 'They's going to destroy them.'

Suddenly, seeing Tam like this, reminded Luke of the ghostly figure he had seen by the Viking ship. Could that have been Tam? Yet Tam was not broad enough across the shoulders. His head was too narrow and his legs slightly bowed.

'Well, there's other ways of doing that. You can

form a protest group. You can go on marches and get people to sign a petition. You can – you can picket, like, stand in the way of the men who come to do the work. That sort of thing.'

'Will it s-save the birds?' asked Tam hopefully.

Luke felt he had to be totally honest with this man, who seemed to take everything at face value.

'I don't know. It does sometimes. Though a lot of the time it doesn't. You see, you can't really fight big firms. They've got too much money. But we could try.'

Tam shook his head slowly. 'It's no good just trying – we've got to get them to go away. If you don't want to help us, then we'll j-j-just have do it on our own, won't we?'

Something prickled in the back of Luke's brain. He tried to tell himself that Tam used 'us' because the man was hoping that other dengies would join him in the fight against the marina. However, the way Tam used the word suggested a more intimate relationship than fellow dengie men. Tam had looked towards the broken mast and nodded, as if the companion of whom he spoke was standing there confirming his words.

'Tam, who's *us*?'

'Us?' repeated Tam.

'What I mean is, who else will help you, if I don't?'

'Why, Svyen of course.'

Luke gulped. 'Svyen?'

Tam suddenly smiled and nodded towards the mast. 'Oh, ah – you can't see him then? I keep forgetting he's a ghost. Svyen is one of the old Viking m-m-men, come over in a long ship. Svyen's been with me since my daddy died. You can't see him then?'

'No,' gulped Luke. 'Not – not this time.'

Tam's eyes lit up.

'You seen Svyen before then?'

'I – I think so.'

Luke stared at the mast. There was no one there. Still, he thought, if someone lived here alone on the marshes he would be bound to be a little mad. Tam had obviously invented an imaginary companion to keep him company during the long, dark, winter days, when there were no twitchers on the marshes. Luke could understand that all right. Yet this did not explain the figure out on the evening marshes.

'What's Svyen doing here? Why's he a ghost?'

Strangely, Luke did not feel as scared as he felt he ought to be on being confronted with a ghost. Perhaps it was because it was daytime and he was in the company of an adult? Or maybe he felt less fear because Tam had just seemed to accept Svyen's ghost as an ordinary part of marsh life?

'He's an old Viking, of course,' cried Tam, triumphantly. 'He drowned away in his b-b-boat, when it sunk. He says to me he wants to go to a place called Valhalla – that's where dead Vikings go to – except he d-drowned.'

'What's drowning got to do with it?' asked Luke.

'Why,' cried Tam, gesturing towards the empty space upon which he said Svyen stood, 'he can't go if he hasn't got his sword in his hand. Vikings n-n-need to have a *weapon* in their hand when they die, otherwise Odin won't let 'em into Valhalla.'

'Is this Valhalla their heaven, or something?'

'It's a place of heroes, see – where all the Viking warriors went when they got killed. Anyways, Svyen will help me, even if you won't. He'll fight for the m-marshes – Vikings don't like buildings and such. They like n-n-natural places.'

'Well, I didn't say I *wasn't* going to help,' Luke argued with Tam. 'I want to help you save the birds, too. It's just a case of finding out the best way to go about it.'

51

Tam smiled again. 'Let's have a cup of tea on it, eh?'

While Luke got dressed again, Tam went into his plywood cabin and boiled an old black kettle on a primus stove. He put a pinch of tea into two bean cans and poured in boiling water. There was no milk or sugar, but though Luke might have complained about that at home, on Tam's boat it felt right.

Luke's can burned his fingers at first, so Tam wrapped a rag round it. Tam himself did not seem to need a rag.

The man and boy sat and sipped the steaming black liquid.

'How do you get money for tea and stuff like that, Tam? You don't go to work, do you?'

'No, I builds bird-watching hides for the twitchers and hires 'em out, see. I puts t-t-tins in the hides with a notice on and they leave me money. They pays me to let 'em sit inside and I uses the money to buy th-things.'

The more Luke spoke to Tam, the more impressed he was with his resourcefulness. Tam was a survivor; he had to be to live out on the marshes alone. Winters here were cruel, the freezing winds coming off the North Sea and sweeping over the flatlands like cold, sharp blades. How Tam kept himself warm under such conditions was a mystery, but perhaps he had taught himself to put up with the cold?

'I'll tell you what we can do,' said Luke, the hot tea burning his food pipe as it went down. 'We can ask the twitchers to help us. *They* won't want the marina here either, will they? I'll come here tomorrow and we can go round and see them together. What do you think?'

'That sounds fine,' said Tam eagerly. 'I'm glad I spoke to you, boy. I don't usually speak to people.'

'Luke – my name's Luke.'

'You're from the Bible, an't you?' Tam said seriously. 'I'm from the Bible, too. My proper name's Thomas and my daddy said I doubted Our Lord's resurrection. But you went to bed with your trousers on, didn't you, Luke?'

'What?' Luke said, mystified.

'You know,' Tam cried, delighted with himself. '*Matthew, Mark, Luke and John, went to bed with their trousers on – one shoe off and one shoe on, Matthew, Mark, Luke and John.*'

'I think you've got the wrong rhyme,' Luke muttered. 'Just like Billy gets the wrong slang words. That's *Diddle-diddle-dumpling, my son John.*'

53

'I learned it from my d-daddy,' smiled Tam.

'Then it's not your fault, is it?' replied Luke.

After they had drunk their tea, Tam led Luke along the secret paths, back to the dyke again. He showed Luke one of his bird-watchers' hides, which was built into the side of a dyke and was hardly visible until you were actually touching it. It was made of old driftwood planks, creosoted and decorated carefully with reeds, shells, seaweed and sun-and-salt-bleached branches. Inside the hide there was enough room for two people to sit on a makeshift bench and stare out through a ten-centimetre slit.

Just inside the door was a small box with a hole in the top, with a very modest amount of money painted crudely on the top of it in red.

Tam told Luke that twitchers could often fool the very shy birds by going in pairs into the hide, then one person leaving shortly afterwards. 'Birds an't very good at sums, they thinks it's all quiet inside.'

'You mean, when they scc only one of the twitchers leave, they believe the hide to be empty?'

'That's it, see – they an't v-v-very good at countin'.'

Luke felt cosy and safe inside the hide, looking

out over the shallows of the marshes where a great variety of waders and shore birds were gathered as if at some political meeting. He recognised wild ducks and geese and, of course, seagulls, but little else. They were making a tremendous noise, all seemingly vying with one another to out-chatter a neighbour, like Prime Minister's Question Time in the House of Commons.

'It's like a birds' parliament,' said Luke, laughing softly. 'All it needs is the party whip.'

Tam, sitting beside him, had his two hands up to his eyes, his fingers curled into tubes like binoculars.

'You got to do this, Luke – or you won't see 'em close.'

Luke laughed again. 'That won't do any good, Tam. You need real binoculars.'

'It does do g-good, it does,' Tam argued firmly. 'I can see them birds much better through 'em.'

So, Luke tried it, and found that he could indeed concentrate better on a single bird or group of birds by looking through pretend binoculars. He realised it was only a way of helping the brain cut out all the other activity on the shallows, but it seemed to work. He watched a bird with long legs and a long downward curving beak strut around and was able to focus his mind on that particular creature alone.

A small bright-blue bird with a spear-point beak flashed past the hide, over the reeds, like a jet fighter plane at an airshow zips over the heads of the crowd.

'What was that?' cried Luke excitedly.

'Kingfisher,' answered Tam promptly. 'Fast, an't he though?'

'Do you get any really *rare* birds here?' asked Luke.

'We had an osprey here, early on,' said Tam proudly.

'What's that? Sounds like a whale or something.'

'It's a fish eagle – big. It d-d-dives like anything for fish and such. She comes down faster than anything with her claws first and catches them f-fish just like that.'

When it was time to go they shook hands. Tam told Luke that Svyen wished him goodbye too. Luke accepted that on face value.

'Why does Svyen want to save the marshes, apart from it being a natural place? I mean, the Vikings destroyed places. They were raiders, weren't they? You know, they robbed the churches and burned down the villages?'

'Svyen – he's been a v-violent man, but he's been

here ever so long now and he's sort of changed a bit, see. You get to learn things when you're as old as him and coming from the sea. Svyen – he likes the birds. When he was alive, he used to watch the birds, to help him know the way home.'

Luke walked back to the cottage. On arrival, his aunt, predictably, wanted to know how his clothes had got so wrinkled. He told her they had been wet and that he had dried them in the sun. She tutted, but Cynthia seldom became upset over such things and it was promptly forgotten.

That evening, out on the garden seat, he told Mary he had met Tam again, and spoken with him. He decided not to tell her about Svyen the Viking for the moment.

'I was on his houseboat thing – it's falling to bits but he doesn't seem to care. I might go there and live with him one day, when I'm over eighteen – if he asks me to, of course. It looks like fun.'

'In the summer it probably is,' said the practical Mary.

'Yeah,' answered Luke, 'I thought of that too. The winter must be really bad. Still, I don't need to stay there in the winter, do I? I can just go when I feel like it.'

Luke didn't say anything to Mary about the

plan to drive off the developers. He didn't want his uncle to know what he was doing and, though he trusted Mary, she might just go and blurt something out by accident. He felt it was best to keep the knowledge to himself for the time being.

Billy came out into the garden and called, 'Your mum's jampot's just got here from London.'

Luke listened and heard a car engine being switched off; he recognised the sound of his mother's old Metro.

'Jam*jar*,' he corrected his young cousin wearily.

When he went indoors he got his hair ruffled immediately and had to suffer a hug from which he extricated himself as soon as he could. His mum was looking good, he had to admit. She had on a new pretty dress and her hair was done up differently. She was full of smiles and the worry lines had gone from her forehead. She said she had found a house in Amersham, but the deal would not go through for a few weeks.

Luke's mother stayed for tea, talking to Joe and Cynthia for an hour or so afterwards. After she had gone, Luke had a talk with his uncle.

'You know the Vikings?' he said.

Joe took his pipe out of his mouth and made a face.

'This is not about that bloomin' ship, is it?'

'No – no, it's about Vikings – the Norse *people*. I mean, you've been here a long time haven't you, Uncle Joe?'

'Not so's I can remember the Vikings,' he chuckled, 'they were before my time.' When he saw that Luke was serious, he continued, 'How long have I been here on the salt marshes? All my life,' said Joe in a satisfied voice. ''Cept when I was away at sea, as a young man – in the merchant marine.'

'Well – well, someone told me that Vikings were interested in birds – like, sea birds. Why would they have been?'

Joe frowned and drew on his pipe, then replied, 'I suspect they used them as navigational aids. If you're out at sea, in a mist or some-at, why, birds will show you which way to go. There's birds that go out to the ocean to fish during the daytime but nest on land at night – so if you watch 'em at evening, you'll know which way lies the land, won't you? You just have to follow their direction, while they're on their way home.'

That made sense to Luke, and birds were part of the environment too. They were part of the natural world that Norsemen knew. The wild and energetic waves, the turbulent skies, the flocks of birds –

59

flights of storm petrels, shearwaters, skuas – all part of a sailor-warrior's life. The Vikings had been close to the elements, closer to the ocean, closer to the land, closer to the creatures of both than modern man.

'So, birds would have been important to a Viking?' Luke said to Joe.

'Undoubtedly, especially the behaviour of sea and salt-marsh birds. Essential part of their lives, prob'ly.'

'So, that's why Svyen is on our side,' murmured Luke, more to himself than the company.

'What?' asked Joe. 'What did you say?'

'Nothing,' replied Luke absently. 'Just thinking.'

5 Svyen likes trouble

Luke was mistaken about his aunt and uncle. They had not left the Quakers. They were highly amused when Luke told them what he had expected them to be wearing and saying, before he had met them.

'Bless you,' said his aunt, 'you're talking about *history*, not now, in the twentieth century. We're just like anybody else, except we don't approve of war . . .'

They asked Luke if he wanted to join Mary and Billy at the local Meeting House that Sunday.

'You don't have to,' said Joe, 'but if you don't, I want you to stay in the house. I don't want you roaming all over the countryside when we're not here. If you had an accident and somebody came for us, why, we wouldn't be here, would we? And they'd accuse us of being neglectful.'

Luke, who did not especially want to stay in the

61

house *or* join his cousins at Quakers, argued with his uncle. 'If I have an accident, I can tell people where you are.'

Billy said, 'You might get hit on the head. A jumbo jet might explode and a toilet might fall out of the sky and bash you on the head – ha, ha. Then you'd be knocked out cold and wouldn't be able to tell anybody, would you? You'd better put on your trumpet and flute and come with us, Luke.'

'It's *whistle* and flute,' growled Luke, grinding his teeth. 'Whistle and flute – *suit*.'

Billy shook his head and looked as serious as a seven-year-old can do sometimes. 'I don't think so, Luke. After all, a whistle isn't a musical instrument, is it? A trumpet is. A trumpet is definitely a musical instrument.'

Luke gave up on that argument. 'I'll watch TV,' he said.

'There's only church services on, anyway,' warned Mary.

So Luke reluctantly accompanied his relatives to the Meeting House and found the service consisted solely of an hour-long silence. It was indeed the longest hour he had ever lived and seemed more than a lifetime. Everyone just sat round an old wooden table on old wooden chairs and either closed their eyes or stared straight ahead of them.

'What are we supposed to be doing?' he whispered to Mary.

'Praying,' she muttered back. 'Or at least, thinking about things to do with the spirit.'

Luke tried that, hoping the time would go faster, but after ten silent, private prayers, which took at *least* half an hour, the big hand on the large railway-station clock situated above his uncle's head had only moved five minutes. Luke was certain the clock had stopped. At least, he corrected himself, not stopped *dead* because it had moved five minutes, but *almost* stopped. It must be slowing to a halt, its works gradually rusting to a final seizure, he thought. He wondered if he ought to tell someone about it, since it appeared nobody had noticed it wasn't working properly.

However, when he glanced down at Mary's watch, he saw that it was indeed only five minutes since he had started his prayers. Incredibly, there was nothing wrong with the clock.

Time passed agonisingly slowly. Even his heart rate had slowed until there were big gaps between each beat. Maybe he was dead, he thought. He tried holding his breath and found he needed oxygen. He

63

almost fell off his chair as he sucked in much needed air noisily at the end of half a minute, incurring a black look from Uncle Joe.

All right, he wasn't dead. But the waiting was pure, undiluted pain. His legs began to twitch with the need to be up and running. He swore that once the hour was over, if it ever did manage to pass during his lifetime, and he was still sane, he would be out of his chair like a bullet from a gun, and wouldn't stop running until he reached the sea.

He *promised* himself that.

There were dull aches in half a dozen places on his body. Every time he moved, even slightly, the chair underneath him creaked loudly. The air was so still he could hear elderly people's stomachs rumbling. He fell into a kind of shallow hibernation; a state of dulled awareness, a dreamless world, hovering on the brink of sleep but never quite falling over the edge. The clock went tick, tick, tick, tick, tick, tick.

'AS I WALKED TO THE MEETING HOUSE THIS MORNING . . .'

Luke's eyes shot open and he almost leaped out of his seat in fright, thinking the thundering voice was that of God. Indeed it was not the Almighty, but one of the Friends who had felt moved to speak and, as was the custom, had risen to his feet and was talking quietly and seriously about a matter which he felt he ought to pass on to other members. His voice was not loud, but the silence had been so deep it had sounded like an earthquake to the unsuspecting Luke.

After the Friend had spoken the silence fell upon them like dust descending from heaven once more, and time slowed down again.

When the big hand on the clock finally reached noon and they had been sitting still for one whole hour, during which stars had been born, flourished and died away to cinders, the Friends suddenly turned to one another, smiled, and shook hands. Luke stretched and yawned, feeling somehow elated. It was as if he had passed a terrible initiation test, like running a gauntlet of clubs or being hung by his heels from a tree, and he now felt he deserved some praise for having made it through the ordeal.

'I was very quiet, wasn't I?' he said to Joe, prompting his uncle to give him his deserved reward.

'Just as you should be,' Joe replied ungratefully. 'The quality of the Silence was good this morning. You're lucky to have come on such a day, Luke.'

Luke stared daggers at his uncle, thinking he

was deliberately being provoked. He had put up with an eternity of discomfort and an agony of boredom. He had put up with his own thoughts for company for a whole hour and found them to be as stale as window-ledge dust, as unpalatable as dead, dry ditch weeds.

'I never thought my head could feel so empty,' he said to Mary.

'That's because you're not used to it,' Mary told him sweetly. 'If you came often you could practise thinking wonderful thoughts.'

'Oh, could I?' he said with sarcasm. 'Like you I suppose?'

'Just like me,' she said, smiling.

Once the family had returned home, Luke was allowed to go roaming over the marshes. It was a dull, listless day that looked as if it wanted to go back to bed again. Luke ran round the dyke to the path which led to Tam's beached ketch. When he reached the gangplank, he hollered, 'You in there, Tam? Can I come aboard?'

Tam peered out shyly through a hole in the marine ply hut.

'A boy,' he said, looking alarmed. 'What shall we d-d-do, Svyen?'

'It's me, Luke,' said Luke, a little disappointed

by the reaction. 'You know me from yesterday. We're going to fight the marina company together, aren't we? To save the birds.'

Tam recognised him then, for he said, 'Oh, it's Luke, Svyen. You remember Luke, don't you? He's going t-t-to help us fight them people. Come over, Luke. I'll make a cup of tea for us.'

Once they had drunk their tea out of the bean cans, Tam said politely, 'You want to see a snake?'

Alarm bells jangled in Luke's brain. He wasn't sure he liked snakes very much.

'Is it poisonous?' he asked.

'Naw, him's only a grass snake.'

Luke breathed deeply to fortify himself, then said, 'All right,' and stood up, expecting to be taken outside.

Instead, Tam lifted another piece of sacking almost at Luke's feet. There, coiled underneath and seemingly asleep, was an eighty-centimetre-long snake with a yellow collar and an olive-green body covered in little black dashes.

Luke moved his feet back quickly. 'You sure it's not dangerous?' he said. 'It looks like an adder to me.' Luke had never actually seen an adder.

'Naw,' smiled Tam. 'I know plenty of them adders – they got black ziggy-zaggy lines down

67

their b-b-backs. This here's a grass snake, see. He won't even bite you if you pick him up. He won't bite you for anything.'

Luke was relieved to hear that, though he had no intention of picking up the sleeping snake. After staring at it for a long while, however, he managed to conquer his fear a little. He kept telling himself he wouldn't be afraid of a cat, which has bigger teeth than the grass snake, so why should he be afraid of something just because it looked slimy?

'Is it slimy?' he asked Tam.

'Naw – he's soft and dry-warm. You touch him – but don't you wake him mind.'

'Why not?' asked Luke, suspiciously.

'Because he's asleep. Bet you don't like to be woke when you sleep. Svyen don't. Svyen hates t-to be woke up when he's fast asleep.'

So Luke carefully reached down and gently stroked the snake's back. It *was* soft and warm. Unfortunately, the grass snake did wake, and moved a little, but it seemed to fall asleep again. Luke was very pleased with himself. He seemed to be passing all the tests with flying colours – first the Quaker Silence – now the marsh snake test.

'They eat frogs and things,' explained Tam. 'They likes water places. He's n-n-not my kept snake. I don't keep the wild things – that's not right. He's just come in here to have him a sleep. Then he'll be off a-hunting f-frogs again.'

'Can you show me some more wild things?' asked Luke, enjoying the idea that he was seeing into a secret world, to which others had no entrance, especially his city pals.

Tam agreed and took Luke out into the dull day. He showed him a hole where adders slept in a great knotted ball during the winter months. Luke shuddered with apprehension. There was a fox's earth on the edge of the marsh, outside which a pile of rubbish had accumulated which the vixen had created herself.

'She just throws it out,' explained Tam. 'Foxes an't the sort to keep the place tidy.'

A weasel was found, and a family of stoats, and a hare's form out on one of the flats. In the main, though, Tam tried to teach Luke the names of the birds that were in evidence in and around the marshes.

The sandpipers, shanks, curlews and godwits were difficult enough to tell apart. There were at least ten types of sandpipers alone. When Luke learned there were *seven* types of thrush, though, he realised how complex the bird world actually was.

Before long he had bird names whizzing around inside his brain like distress rockets.

'Those are crows, aren't they?' he said, pointing to some big black birds which had exploded from a tall spinney.

'Naw, them's *rooks*. Crows stay by themselves, mostly – they don't go in for living together.'

'Ah,' said Luke, 'you mean like *you're* a crow.'

Tam smiled, shyly. 'That's right. I don't like living with other people. I likes it on my own.'

Whenever the pair came across twitchers, Luke would go up to them and introduce himself. Then he would ask the twitchers if they would sign a petition against the marshes being taken over by the marina company. Almost to a person the twitchers agreed that the marshes should stay as they are, a sanctuary for the many birds that inhabited them. Luke promised to return during the next week with the petition.

One man he spoke to sighed deeply. 'I'll sign your petition, but I think you've got a terrible fight on your hands. The man who owns that company is Jason Pritchard, one of the wealthiest developers in the country. He's got a dozen lawyers working for him. Who have you got?'

Luke blinked and scratched his head. 'Just me

and Tam – Tam's that man over there. He's a dengie.'

'Then I don't give much for your chances. I'd like to help, but I'm leaving the country myself on Tuesday, for Saudi Arabia. If I were you, I'd get some big guns on your side. What about writing to the RSPB – the Royal Society for the Protection of Birds?

'Well, yes, I'll do that all right,' said Luke.

'Other than that, you might need an army to keep Pritchard out of here. I've dealt with him myself. The man's a predator when he sees a profit in front of him. He'll just go in for the kill and the environment be damned.'

When Luke went back to Tam with this information, Tam's response was to go back for his gun.

'You *can't* go threatening people with guns, Tam. Whatever you do, you can't do that. Let's see if we can get some lawyers on our side. There must be lawyers who're twitchers, mustn't there? Let's ask a few of them if they can help us, eh?'

Tam agreed miserably to go along with Luke's plans, but he clearly lacked any confidence in the scheme.

'Svyen says we ought to fight.'

Luke looked automatically at the spot in the

bows of the old boat where Tam had told him Svyen usually stood guard. The sunlight in that quarter was bright and strong, and heat waves shimmered from the deckboards making the insects glitter and the dust in the air sparkle. It seemed to form a kind of wavering spectral image. Luke was not sure whether he could see anything there or not. It was probably another one of those strange tricks of the light that had him wondering.

'Well, Svyen's wrong this time; fighting will just bring us trouble.'

Tam stared at Luke, then at the bows of the boat.

Then the hermit turned and bent over to whisper in Luke's ear. 'Problem is, Svyen *likes* trouble.'

6 Raiders in the evening

Finding someone sympathetic to their cause was easy for Luke and Tam, but finding someone who would actually *help* them proved to be hopeless. The twitchers all said they would write to various bodies like the RSPB and RSPCA, but they themselves were too busy to become involved. Luke also wrote to the RSPB, but time was getting short. Jason Pritchard's men were already arriving in heavy lorries and unloading large sections of pipe.

'Svyen wants to know what's them for?' asked Tam. 'Them pipe things?'

'I think they'll be used to drain the marshes,' said Luke, grimly, as the pair of them watched the unloading operation from behind a dyke. 'They've got to get rid of the water before they can start digging out the marina.'

Tam was quiet for a minute, then he said

quietly, 'Svyen says we got t-t-to smash them pipes to bits.'

The ghost which Tam said kept him company seemed to Luke to be forever wanting to do battle. Luke looked around nervously for signs of the invisible Viking. He could see nothing but the wind stirring the grasses. He could hear nothing but the cry of the sea birds. He could smell nothing but the salt air, the creek mud and the estuary water-margin plants. It was a pity he could not talk to Svyen himself, but Tam had told him that a person had to spend a lifetime on the marshes before he was able to talk with its ghosts.

Yet, Svyen was exactly the kind of creature Luke would expect of a Viking ghost. Svyen was, after all, a warrior. It had been Svyen's job to demolish things. That was what the Norsemen had been good at: slaughtering people and destroying their villages and towns. It wouldn't do here though.

'That's all right for a Viking – they went around smashing things all the time – but we might get put in prison for it, Tam. I don't think it's a good idea.'

Tam shook his head in a determined way. 'Look at what them men are doing now . . .'

Luke looked and saw that Pritchard's men were

erecting a barbed-wire fence round a section on the edge of the marshes, inside which they were building a small hut. Also within the confines of the fence they were placing large pieces of equipment: diggers, cranes, pumps, dumpers. Indeed, they looked as if they were going to transform the landscape in a serious way.

'What's that small house for?' asked Tam.

Luke sighed. 'It's probably so that they can leave a man behind to guard the equipment – a security man. Look, they're putting up lights round the fence now. There's no way we're going to be able to get in there and wreck those pipes.'

'I can d-do it,' said Tam in a determined voice. 'Svyen says so. Svyen says we got to save the birds – they's part of his soul, he says, like the marsh itself. Once you start killin' innocent creatures and tearin' up the land, then things start to fall to bits and disappear into nothin'.'

A herring gull carked as if to confirm Tam's words.

Luke rolled over and lay in the grass, staring at the white clouds floating through the blueness above. It was a deep hard sky that day.

A large grey heron sailed overhead, probably on its way to pillage some garden pond of its silver and gold fish, just as the Vikings had robbed the English churches of their treasures long ago. Luke turned his head towards the marshland where the morning mist was still clinging to the creeks and, where the sunlight slanted through the reeds, he thought he saw a moving shadow. He stared hard, trying to make out some shape from the light and shade. An idea had occurred to him which he might have dismissed as silly another time, but now he was desperate for some answer to their problem.

'Hey!' cried Luke, sitting up. 'Will you talk to Svyen for me, Tam?'

Tam looked doubtful. 'I can t-try – if he'll listen, Luke.'

'Can you ask him if he drowned when his long-boat sank in this river?' asked Luke eagerly.

Tam replied, 'Svyen heard you, and he says, yes – he drowned right away, in the cold waters of this here River Roach, when he was not more than twenty-four winters in age. His ship hit something – maybe some tree spikes left by the English people – and sank down deep in the tide.'

'I think I saw his ship,' said Luke excitedly. 'It was in one of the creeks. If we could find it, maybe Jason Pritchard wouldn't be able to build his marina here? The museum people probably wouldn't let him – not until they got the boat out. That would give us some more time, wouldn't it? Do you remember seeing an old wreck Tam – a *Viking* wreck?'

Tam shook his head slowly. 'I an't seen nothing like that in the creeks.'

'Well, I wasn't seeing things. I know it's there somewhere. Ask Svyen where he drowned.'

Tam was quiet for a moment, then he looked at Luke with sad eyes.

'Svyen can't tell. He can't say things like where his b-b-boat sunk.'

That was just great. Svyen was quick to give advice about smashing private property, but ask him something important and he hedged. That was just typical of the Viking ghost.

Surely, thought Luke, if he himself had seen the hulk just one day after he had moved to Paglesham, then Tam, who had lived on the marshes all his life, *must* have seen it at some time. If Luke could make Tam feel that proof of his ghost's existence depended upon his answer, then he might reach into his own memory and dredge something up.

Tam looked frustrated. 'He can't tell us,' he shouted, making some of the workmen turn their heads and stare. 'Svyen can't tell us.'

77

Luke said quietly, 'All right, all right, Tam – I believe you. Look, I *know* I saw a ship, but it wasn't there the next day when I took my uncle. What's the reason for that, eh? Can you just answer me that?'

Tam did not appear to be listening. Instead, he was staring angrily at the lorries continually arriving on the edge of the marshes. Then he turned to Luke and said, 'You coming with me and Svyen tonight? To smash them pipes with us? Eh, Luke?'

'I – I don't know, Tam. It's dangerous.'

'We'll smash them pipes, but we won't wait on you, if you don't come. Midnight, see.'

That evening, at home, Luke spoke to his uncle about Jason Pritchard's men unloading their equipment.

Joe said, 'I heard about that – they didn't waste no time. We all put in our objections, to the council, but they say they can't do nothing about it. Central government's encouraging this sort of enterprise, so they said. It's seen as good business to bring jobs. I'm not so sure though. I think once it's been built and we've lost our marshes, there won't be but two or three people needed to run the marina. Manager types – not people from the village, that's for sure.'

Mary said, hotly, 'It'll affect the whole ecological balance of the region.'

Joe looked with obvious pride at his daughter. 'Ecological balance. That's the ticket. One of the Paglesham Residents Committee – Mrs Doubly from Churchend – she's going to see the council tomorrow. But she said not to hold our breath. She's been before and they weren't altogether helpful. Maybe you should go with her, Mary.'

'I will,' said Mary.

Later, lying uneasily in his bed, Luke started to worry about Tam, because if Tam were caught he might be sent to jail, and prison might drive a man like Tam insane. He had spent all his life thus far in absolute freedom and to lock him up behind bars would be like shutting a heron in an orange box.

When Luke was sure Billy had fallen asleep, he crept out of bed and quietly got dressed. Next, he crept downstairs and went to the cupboard in the kitchen where Cynthia kept a torch ready for emergencies. He left the house by the back door, making sure he left it unlocked. His feet sounded loud on the gravel road, as he crunched his way carefully to the footpath which led to the dyke. Once the house was out of sight behind some trees he switched on the torch and let out a sigh of relief.

Luke made his way to the dyke and from there to Tam's barge. As he approached the sunken vessel he could see it was in darkness. He called out: 'Tam? Are you there?'

There was no answer. Luke realised it was quite late and, though Tam had said he would wait until midnight, the dengie had no means of telling the time except by the movements of the tide – and perhaps the moon, planets and stars. No doubt Tam could judge it to within half-an-hour or so, but that would be the extent of his accuracy.

Luke ran quickly back down the path and then along the dyke to the place where the pair of them had been spying on Jason Pritchard's men that afternoon. When he looked towards their fence, he could see the perimeter lights were blazing, creating a halo of brightness round the site. Everything looked peaceful and still. There was another light on, inside the hut.

While Luke was staring, there was a movement down by the lights. He peered carefully at the spot and saw Tam. The dengie man was crawling through the grasses, edging his way towards the site. Luke crept down the dyke and into those same grasses, following Tam's example.

Being smaller and more agile, Luke was able to catch up with Tam, who heard him coming. The tall man turned with round eyes full of fear, which soon changed to smiles.

'You came?' he whispered. 'Svyen said you w-would, but I din't believe him.'

'Yes,' said Luke, still not sure he was doing the right thing. 'I came. Is Svyen here?'

'He's standing next to you, Luke.'

Luke looked round nervously to find the grasses flattened in various places. Svyen could have been in any one of a number of spots.

Tam led the way to the fence. When he reached it he didn't try to climb it. Instead, he scraped away the earth from underneath with his thin hands. Like a fox entering a chicken run, Tam dug a small gap under the wire, then wriggled through it. With his heart pounding in his chest, Luke followed. They both emerged on the other side without rousing the night-watchman. Still swallowing his fear, Luke ducked down behind a mechanical shovel. He took several deep breaths, gathering together his courage, wondering what Tam had in mind to keep the night-watchman from discovering them.

There was a bale of wire left over from stringing the fence that day. It leaned against the wall of the hut. Tam stealthily crept over to this and picked it up. Keeping below the window line he went round to the front of the hut and wound the wire round the door handle. Then he proceeded to stalk round the hut several times, still keeping his body below the line of sight from whoever was within. Finally, he hooked the wire round the door handle again.

The occupant of the hut was securely bound inside. The windows were too small for an adult to squeeze through. Tam had effectively immobilised the night-watchman.

Next, Tam went to the gate. Near to the track there was a pile of thick iron rods for reinforcing concrete. Tam picked up one of these and attacked the gate, breaking it from its hinges. The noise he made caused a commotion from inside the hut.

'Hey, what's going on?' someone tried the door of the hut and found it would not open.

'HEY! HEY!' the night-watchman yelled, kicking at the door with his boots.

'Quick,' cried Tam. He rushed outside the compound and began smashing the perimeter lights with his iron bar. Until then Luke had felt as if he were in some kind of exciting game, but now his knees almost buckled under him in fright as the man in the hut began screaming obscenities, telling them he was calling the police. Luke guessed the man had a mobile phone in there, though he was actually still pounding on the door, trying to break out.

Once the lights were all out, the place was lit only by the glow from the hut windows, and from the moon.

A pipe suddenly slid and rolled from the top of a pile and smashed to the ground. Then another came tumbling down. Luke and Tam were nowhere near the pipes, in fact, Luke was having second thoughts about damaging private property, yet here were the pipes breaking *themselves*. Or was someone else there, someone unseen, who was impatient to get things started?

'Oh, well,' said Luke, 'I'm in it now. Even if I don't do anything, they'll never believe the pipes broke on their own.'

He grabbed one of the iron bars and began smashing the ceramic pipes. His fright turned his actions into frenzied movements as he ran from one pile of pipes to another, wielding the weapon. Tam joined him. The noise was terrible, what with the night-watchman yelling and pounding, and the pipes shattering. Luke had the impression that someone else was breaking pipes, as well as him and Tam.

'They'll get dogs after this,' said Luke breathlessly. 'They'll get savage Dobermans or something.'

'I can talk to dogs,' said Tam, and, unlike his reaction to the ghost, this time Luke believed him.

Once the pipes had been destroyed, Luke and Tam began to stuff mud into the petrol tanks of the vehicles in the yard: the mechanical diggers, the dumper truck and other machinery. The hut had gone ominously quiet and when Luke looked up next he saw the man trying to shine a torch on them through one of the small windows, presumably so that he could recognise them again.

Luke ducked under the sweeping beam and warned Tam to do the same. Tam was not so quick and got caught in the light. Then came the sound of engines from beyond the marshes. Luke recognised them as the sound of Ford motor-cars, the kind often used by the police. This was confirmed shortly afterwards as a siren was switched on.

'The Old Bill!' cried Luke. 'They're coming!'

The pair of them ran through the gateway. Tam dropped his iron bar, but Luke had the presence of mind to pick it up again. Once they were on the dyke, Luke threw both the bars into the mud where they sank out of sight in a creek.

'They could've got our fingerprints,' he hissed at the not-so-worldly Tam.

Tam said, 'Me fingers is covered in mud from digging,' which was true enough. Luke's weren't, though, and he was glad he had thought to get rid of the bars.

They hurried along the bottom edge of the dyke, using the moonlight to guide their feet, just as the police pulled up on the edge of the marshes. Birds called out in the darkness of the creeks, disturbed by their presence. A fox glided by them in the opposite direction, as surprised as they were by the night encounter. A nightjar flew up from a hollow.

There was a lot of shouting coming from behind them and torches cut through the night like search-lights, but Luke knew the police stood little chance of catching them now. When they reached the place where Tam had to part with him, Luke said, 'Don't worry – they didn't see us.'

'He saw me,' nodded Tam.

'They've still got to find out who you are and where you come from,' said Luke. 'Just lie low.'

With that, Luke left his friend and hurried back along the dyke to the cottage. His throat was dry, but his mind was clear and sharp. The shock of what he had done made his skin tingle and his heart skip faster. He was a criminal.

Thankfully, the door was still unlocked when he arrived and he pushed it open gently – only to find himself confronted by an astonished Mary, who was getting herself a cool drink from the refrigerator.

'Where have you been?' she enquired.

'Shhhhh! I've – I've been out somewhere – a walk. I had to go for a walk.'

'Oh yes?' she said, raising her eyebrows. 'And what were the police sirens for? They woke me up.'

'I haven't been burglaring,' whispered Luke fiercely. 'I've been – been doing something else.'

'It's *burgling* and you'd better tell me what you've been up to, if you don't want my mum and dad down here.'

Luke was scared and frustrated. The sweat on his brow and the look on his face were enough to tell Mary he hadn't just been for a stroll. He had no choice. He told Mary everything, in about three minutes flat. Then he waited.

7 The Quaker way

'You're a saboteur,' whispered Mary, her censure mingled with traces of admiration and awe.

'A reluctant one,' squirmed Luke. 'Very reluctant.'

'I bet you destroyed all the machinery on their site. That could cost tens of thousands of pounds. You might end up paying for the rest of your life, Luke.'

'Thank you, Mary,' he said, bitterly. 'You're really good at cheering people up. Anyway, we didn't destroy the machinery – we just put mud in the petrol tanks. We only smashed up the piping.'

'That's bad enough, isn't it? It's still other people's property.'

Feeling dreadfully thirsty, Luke grabbed the lemonade bottle she was holding and took a long swig. Then he handed it back to her, wiping his mouth on the back of his hand. She looked at the neck of the bottle with an offended expression on her face.

'I'm not going to drink from that *now*. It's unhygienic. Men are such disgusting creatures sometimes. Listen, I'm not going to help you and Tam Goodson with your sabotage, but I will help you talk to people. Negotiation is the only way to solve things in this world, not violent action.'

'Talk never did any good.'

'It depends how it's done,' replied Mary. 'You just want to have fun breaking things.'

'Fun?' he almost yelled. 'It's not *fun*. It's flippin' dangerous. If we get caught we'll go to prison.'

'Don't be daft, they don't send kids to prison for things like that. You'll probably just go to a juvenile correction centre.'

The sweat broke out on Luke's brow again. 'And that's not just as bad? I'll get corrupted by *real* criminals. Kids who deal in drugs, steal cars and mug people. I'll be hooked on crime for the rest of my life.'

Mary giggled. 'You do exaggerate, Luke.'

At that moment Billy entered the room, rubbing his eyes. 'What are you two squirrelling about?' he yawned. 'You woke me up.'

'Rabbiting, the word is rabbiting,' hissed Luke. 'If you don't get this slang right, I'll go bonkers.'

Billy stared at his cousin. 'Why are you dressed, Luke? You going out?'

'Yes, yes I was. I was going out for a stroll along the country lanes. I just woke up and felt like a long walk in the middle of the night. Don't reckon I'll go now, though – not now the world and his wife is up and about. Think I'll just go up the old apples and plums and back to bed.'

'Apples and *pears*, Luke. Get it right,' admonished Billy.

'Apples and grapes, apples and apricots, apples and flippin' bananas,' growled Luke. 'If you can do it, so can I.' Then he marched out of the kitchen and up the stairs, got undressed and went to bed. He fell into a troubled sleep from which he did not wake until eleven o'clock.

'You're up late this morning, Luke – I couldn't wake you,' said his aunt.

'I – I was kept awake by some police sirens,' said Luke. 'Dunno what was going on. It was two before I managed to get to sleep . . .'

His aunt seemed to accept this explanation, telling him someone had broken into the Sintra Marina site during the night and caused a lot of damage. Luke had a piece of toast, then left the house. He headed straight for Tam's place, but as he hurried along the dyke he ran straight into Mary and Johnny Elms. Mary said to Johnny, 'I'm going with Luke now – I promised to show him something.'

Johnny made a face, then said to Luke, 'I bet it was you.'

Luke coloured up and said, 'What?' in a high-pitched voice.

'So it *was* you what broke into the builders' site yesterday – broke all them things.'

Mary said, 'Luke's not the sort of person who goes around breaking other people's property.'

Johnny turned on her. 'You would say that, wouldn't you? Protecting *him*. Well, I know it was you and I'm going to spread it around, so whatcha goin' to do about *that* then, eh?'

'I might whack you one,' said Luke, bunching his fingers into a fist.

'Like to see you try, snotnose,' Johnny said, stepping forward.

Luke squared up to his opponent, his heart beating faster in his chest. There was a contained anger within him, mostly directed at himself for getting involved in the previous evening's escapades. A fight was just the thing for getting rid of bottled vexation.

'Johnny Elms, if you don't leave us alone, I'll never speak to you again – ever,' said Mary. 'I mean it.'

Johnny looked at her and, reluctantly it seemed, backed off a few paces.

'And you'd better not go spreading lies around, Johnny Elms, or I'll get my dad to see your dad. That's slanderous behaviour, that is, and you can be prosecuted for slanderous behaviour. Just bear that in mind before you start accusing people without proof.'

'You're too clever for your own good, Mary Jackson,' Johnny growled, then he turned on his heel and left them.

'Now,' said Mary, 'let's go and see Tam – that's where you were going, wasn't it?'

'Mary . . .' began Luke, but she wasn't listening. She was stepping out in front, leading the way.

Luke followed his stubborn cousin as she walked along the top of the dyke. The sea lavender was in full bloom and its tangy fragrance wafted up from the beds of flowers in the creeks. This had a calming effect on Luke's anger, but he still feigned annoyance with Mary for stopping the fight.

'You should have let me thump him,' he said.

'I'm a Quaker. We don't believe in violence.'

'You believe in helping saboteurs though,' muttered Luke.

'That depends,' she said. 'Quakers believe in negotiation.' She sighed, before adding, 'The trouble is, Jason Pritchard won't listen. He just bulldozes ahead.'

'Bulldozes, that's a good word,' Luke said, in a sarcastic tone.

'You mean appropriate,' said Mary over her shoulder. 'Yes, I thought it was pretty smart too.'

Luke fumed, thinking she really was the most maddening person.

The mud was rich in birds this morning, with plovers and sandpipers forming the largest groups. There were oyster-catchers out there, too, looking for shellfish on a shoreline teeming with life. There were curlews stalking amongst the yellow-flowering sea purslane and warblers hiding amongst the reeds and grasses in and alongside the dyke. Luke could imagine just how many birds would suffer if the marina were built.

When they got to Tam's hulk, Tam himself was nowhere to be seen, so they settled down and waited for him. It was a sunny day again and, without any effort whatsoever, Luke fell asleep in an old deckchair. He was woken by Mary, who shook him hard.

'Tam's back,' she said.

Tam was standing there with a long face. He had dark streaks down his cheeks and had clearly been crying. Luke had never seen a grown man cry. It worried him and took away his confidence.

'What's the matter, Tam?' Mary was saying. 'Come on, you know me – I'm Mary from the cottages at Eastend, aren't I? What's happened. Did anyone hurt you?'

'Them men,' said Tam in a mournful voice. 'They chased me and Svyen, they did. Then they – they smashed them bird hides – smashed 'em all to bits.'

Jason Pritchard's men could not have found a more effective way of hurting the tall, quiet man if they had sat down for a thousand years and thought about it.

Mary said in a shocked voice, 'They can't do that.'

'They did it, they did it,' said Tam. 'They shouted after me. They told me the hides was illegal and they was acting out the law, they did. Svyen's n-n-not happy. He's very unhappy, he is – v-very unhappy.'

Luke, in an aside, began to explain about Svyen, but she knew about him.

'All the kids know about Svyen and Tam. He talks to an imaginary person sometimes, to tell people things without actually talking to them properly.'

Unlike Mary, Luke was of the opinion that Tam could see things others could not.

'What does Svyen say about the marina now?'

'Why,' Tam said fiercely, 'he tells me we must do more to stop those men from chasing away our birds.'

'He – he doesn't say you should stop?'

'Svyen likes to fight,' said Tam. 'He's standing next to you with his big helmet shining in the s-s-sun and his sword is out of its sheath thing. He's got his blue cloak on, which means his mad is up and he wants to fight someone.'

Luke glanced nervously, first one side and then the other, seeing nothing.

Mary said, 'Early this morning I went to town with Mrs Doubly, to see the council. They said they can't do anything to stop Jason Pritchard from building his marina. It's up to us now. But we mustn't use violence, Tam – we mustn't hurt people. And we mustn't destroy things.'

'How are we going to do it then,' asked Luke helplessly, 'if we're not supposed to break things?'

'When they put the pipes down,' Mary explained, 'we'll block them with clay. It won't damage the machinery, but they won't be able to drain the marshes, will they? If the weather stays like this, the clay will bake hard inside the pipe. Clay can get like concrete, you know. They used to make bricks out of clay baked in the sun.'

Tam blinked and said to Luke, 'Svyen wants to know if it will work all right.'

'Mary's right, you know. Smashing things will only get us into serious trouble. We have to think of ways to stop them without actually doing any damage. Blocking the pipes is good.'

Tam replied, 'Svyen says Mary is a great w-w-warrior.'

Luke was a big piqued by this statement. *He* was the one who had stood shoulder to shoulder with Tam and battled against the Pritchard empire. He was the one wanted by the police and Jason Pritchard's men. Not Mary. Mary hadn't done anything yet – nothing worth speaking about.

'How can a *girl* be a great warrior?' Luke sniffed. 'In history . . .'

'In history,' said Mary, 'there was Queen Boudicca who fought the Romans, there was Joan of Arc, there was Cleopatra, there was Alexandress the Great.'

'Alexandress the Great?' squeaked Luke, raising his eyebrows.

'Just testing you,' smiled Mary smugly. 'Anyway, now there's Mary of Paglesham, like it or lump it, Luke Tynan.'

'I'll lump it,' he muttered.

They stayed with Tam the rest of the afternoon. Tam showed them how to lay band lines for fish out in the muddy creek when the tide was low, with a dozen hooks dangling from one piece of line stretched between two posts.

'But you got to stay with them lines 'til they're covered with water, otherwise them gu-gu-gulls eat up the bait. Then you got to be waitin' when the tide goes out, just the same, or them gulls eat the fish you caught.'

Just as the sun was weakening in the later afternoon and the newts were coming up around the boat looking for insects on the surface of the water, Luke and Mary said goodbye to Tam.

'When are we goin' to block the pipes?' asked Tam, before they left.

'They haven't laid them yet,' said Mary. 'I expect some new ones will arrive today, to replace those you broke, so they'll probably start tomorrow. Maybe we can do it tomorrow evening, or the evening after. We'll have to play it by ear.'

'What ear?' Tam asked, looking puzzled.

'Never mind, I'll tell you,' said Mary. 'And in the meantime I'll try to think of some more things we can do, to frustrate them. All right?'

The two cousins left Tam standing on the deck of his houseboat and made their way through the marsh paths to the dyke. There, waiting on the dyke was a familiar figure. Luke sighed and shook his head.

'I'm not fighting you, Johnny Elms – I've turned into a Quaker.'

'Don't want to fight,' said Johnny. 'I just want to join your gang.'

'What gang?' asked Mary.

'The gang you three have got, to wreck Jason Pritchard's marina.'

'Don't know what you're talking about,' Luke said.

'Come off it,' said Johnny Elms. 'You know. If

you don't let me join, I'll cause trouble, OK? And see, if you do, it'll be one more on your side, won't it?' he added plaintively.

He stood there awaiting their decision and eventually Mary said, 'Oh, all right, you're in.'

'Hey, wait a minute?' cried Luke. 'Don't I get a say?'

Mary stared at him. 'Well?' she said.

Luke said weakly, 'Er, yeah, after careful consideration – you're in, Johnny Elms.'

Johnny grinned and held out his hand. Luke grinned and shook it. Mary rolled her eyes heavenward.

8 Raiders in the night

Just as Mary had predicted, the new pipes arrived on the following day and the three children stood and watched them being unloaded. That afternoon they went to visit Tam, to see if he had recovered from the shock of having his hides destroyed.

Tam was sitting on the deck of his hulk, carefully and gently unwinding a tangle of fishing line from the legs of a wild-eyed godwit. The bird was submissive enough, but it looked terrified. Tam kept stroking the creature and speaking to it in a tender voice to try to calm its fears. Luke, Mary and Johnny sat on the opposite bank until Tam had finished. Finally the nylon line was disentangled and the godwit flew free.

Mary said, 'These fishermen should be more careful – sometimes they just cut away a tangle from their fishing line and let it drop into the grasses. Same with hooks and weights. Birds get caught by them and die – even big birds, like swans.'

Tam was surprised to see yet another young person involved in the fight against Jason Pritchard, but he was getting used to them just arriving unannounced at his home. He made some tea and then got a bit flustered because he only had three empty bean cans, until Johnny offered to share his with Mary, who gracefully accepted but pointedly drank from the opposite side of the can with a fastidious expression on her face.

Johnny said, 'Hey, you've got a fantastic place here, Tam – this was probably a pirate ship or something.'

Mary said, 'Never mind the boy, his imagination runs a little wild sometimes.'

Then they got down to making plans for the following evening. Besides an almanac, Mary had brought a map with her: the Ordnance Survey Sheet TQ 89/99 1:25000. As it was large scale she was able to pinpoint the likely locations of the piping which would be used to drain the marshes.

'We've got to be sure where we're going,' she said, 'because we won't be able to use torches. They'll be watching for us this time and torches will be seen. I've looked in the almanac and there'll be a moon, providing the weather isn't bad, which it doesn't look like being according to the forecast. It'll be high tide, so they won't be pumping the water from the marshes – they can only do that on to the mud flats at low tide.'

Tam did not understand the map or almanac, but he knew what Mary was talking about and he added a piece himself.

'There'll prob'ly be a bit of a flooding in the creeks tomorrow night,' he said. 'It's a big tide.'

'How's that?' asked Luke.

Mary had been glancing at her almanac. 'You're right, Tam,' she said excitedly. 'There'll be a sort of eclipse – which will cause greater gravitational pull on the oceans.'

'What's that mean?' asked Johnny. 'In plain English.'

'The moon's partly responsible for the tides,' answered Mary. 'If the pull is stronger, the tide is higher. You think it's going to come over the dykes, Tam?'

Tam nodded. 'The creatures think so. Some of 'em are moving back a bit from the river. The crickets is talking to each other about it, too. Big tide,

101

they says. They told Svyen and me about a high water.'

Johnny glanced enquiringly at Luke, who in turn widened his eyes as if to say, Your guess is as good as mine.

'How does that help us?' asked Luke. 'I mean, with our plan?'

Mary said, 'It means there'll be confusion around, quite a few people, like coastguards, lifeboatmen, nervous yachtsmen moving their expensive white boats to safer moorings. Stuff like that. Last time the dyke was breached they had to bring in lorry loads of sandbags to plug the gap.'

'Hadn't we better warn somebody, then?' said Luke.

Mary said, 'They'll know there's a high tide coming, same as we do. That's what the almanac's for – so that people know what might happen in the future. They'll have people standing by, ready to evacuate us if its necessary.'

'Then we won't be able to plug the pipes,' said Luke.

'We'll do it before the floodtide. There's a good chance the dykes won't be breached anyway. It doesn't happen *every* time there's a small eclipse.

More often than not it comes and goes without any damage being caused.'

No one came to evacuate them during the late evening. When Mary and Luke crept from their beds and went outside into the night, they could hear the sounds of the river traffic in progress. They went to the garden shed and got themselves a trowel each, to help with digging the clay.

It was obvious from the amount of activity on the water that the authorities were well aware of a special tide in progress. Mary had told Luke that on waterways over the whole country there were marker posts with scales that helped the authorities monitor the progress of an unusually high tide.

'I hope it doesn't get too bad,' said Mary, as they crept through the garden gate, 'otherwise the cottages will be in danger.'

'And us!' Luke said, alarmed.

'Yeah,' said a voice behind him. 'An' Mum and Dad will wake up and find us gone.'

The voice electrified both Luke and Mary. They turned to see that they had been followed by Billy. He was fully dressed.

'Where d'you think you're going?' hissed Mary.

'With you two,' said Billy. 'You're my china dishes.'

'China *plates* – mates,' growled Luke.

Mary tried to reason with Billy. 'Look, you're not old enough to come with us, Billy. You'll fall asleep or get caught or something. Mum and Dad will have a fit if they find you've been out.'

'They'll have a fit if they find *you've* been out,' replied Billy, with some justification. 'I'm comin' and that's that!'

Mary and Luke knew they were stuck with him. If they didn't let him come he would make a fuss and wake Joe and Cynthia. Luke shrugged, help-lessly, and Mary sighed.

'All right,' she whispered, 'but you've got to do as you're told for once – and stop teasing Luke with that silly cockney rhyming slang.'

Luke was incensed. 'You mean he's doing it on purpose?' But by that time, Mary and Billy were striding out along the flint track to the dyke. Luke caught up with them. As they neared the dyke Luke could see something shining, like silver, on the top of the dyke. He pointed it out to Mary.

'What is it?' he hissed.

Mary stared for a while. There were more sounds coming to them now, carried on the soft night air. A buoy was clanging in the far distance. Foghorn moans were wafting up from the south, sounding to Luke like the groans of unhappy ghosts. There was a sense of movement and quiet urgency on the many rivers which cut Essex into horizontal strips: the Thames to the south, the Blackwater, Colne and Stour to the north, the Crouch into which their River Roach flowed. It seemed to him that, on the moonlit land and sea-scape, there was a nightworld in motion.

Mary replied to his question. 'It's water – that shining stuff. The tide's come right up to the top of the dykes. The creeks must be brim full.'

The three children stared in awe at the high tide, held back from flooding their home only by the tall dykes that lay like lazy giant snakes on and around the marshlands.

Mary looked at her watch in the moonlight. 'Well,' she said, relieved, 'it won't get any higher. It should be on the turn now.'

'Good job,' said Billy. 'Otherwise they'd have come round and woken Mum and Dad – then where would we be, eh?'

'I wonder they haven't woken people already,' said Luke, 'with it being that high.'

'Happens every year, once or twice,' said Mary.

'You can't evacuate people unless there's *really* going to be a flood, can you?'

Luke supposed not. There was a creaking sound now and the slapping of sheets against wood. He stared upwards when a ketch leaned over them, high above, as it steered close to the bank. The rigging lights glittered, mingling with the stars. It seemed as if the craft were about to fall on their heads from the heavens. Then the sail flapped away from them as the boat gybed, tacking out towards the middle of the river.

Just then a new danger threatened. Car headlights suddenly swept along the track. An engine growled.

'Quick,' cried Luke, 'the police. Into the bushes.'

The three kids scrambled into the hedgerow and crouched down, just as a car cruised along the track and up to the foot of the dyke.

Two policemen got out of the car and climbed up the bank to stare out over the river. They stood there, muttering to one another in voices too low for the children to hear what was being said. Mary and Billy settled down comfortably and seemed happy to wait until the police had gone. The police remained on top of the dyke for twenty minutes.

Normally Luke would have been twitching and

straining at an invisible leash within five minutes in such a position, but, what would have previously seemed an eternity to him was now a short period of time. Mary and Billy of course were completely used to the silent hour of sitting still which they practised almost every week. Luke had done it once, and that single agonising hour of letting time click by, second by second, helped him enormously.

Finally, the policemen came down from the dyke, got in their car, and drove back along the flint track.

'How did you know that was the cops?' asked Billy. 'They didn't have their flashing lights on.'

'I guessed,' confessed Luke. 'Police cars are nearly always Fords. Anyway, I heard them the other night when Tam and I were running away from Pritchard's site. Car engine sounds are like people's voices to me – once I've heard one I can recognise it again.'

'That's *clever*,' said Mary, sounding impressed, which made Luke feel really good.

Knowing they had already wasted a lot of time, Luke suggested they get moving. They climbed up on to the dyke and began running alongside the high water, noting the abnormal amount of busy, light-encrusted river traffic, where people were moving their boats back from safe havens to their normal mooring places. At any other time the kids would have found the scene fascinating, but now they had a job to do.

They found Johnny by one of the concrete pill-boxes, where he said he would be, and Tam had come up to the dyke further along. Tam told them his Thames barge was half-floating and half-flooded in the high creek waters, but it was securely moored so nothing much could happen to it. When the waters subsided the boat would settle in a new position on the mud. It would dry out over the rest of the summer.

The whole gang then made their way to the temporary pumping station which Pritchard's men had established on the edge of the marshes. Twin pipe-lines now left this site and were already halfway to the river. The pumps were silent now at high water, but, once the tide had ebbed, the rest of the pipes would fit into place and the draining of the marshes would begin.

Except for the marshy areas, the region was part of the London basin, formed of thick clay. It was Mary's idea that they find the open end of the pipes and stuff clay into them, to well and truly clog them. They would follow the glittering twin pipes to the place where they rose on trestles, up towards the river walls. At the end of the trail the snouts of the pipes looked like twin cannons about to discharge their missiles at the residents of villages on the far side of the river.

The whole area, however, was enclosed by a three-metre high chainlink fence. The top of the fence was protected by rolls of deadly looking razor wire; impossible to climb over. The bottom was securely staked to the ground, to prevent intruders from digging underneath it, as Tam had done on their previous mission to smash the ceramic pipes.

'How are we going to get in *there*?' groaned Luke. 'It's like a fortress!'

9 Forces of the law

'It does look a bit difficult,' said Mary.

'Difficult?' exploded Luke. 'It's hopeless. We'd need to have wire cutters to get into that place!'

'You mean, like these?' said Johnny, producing an object from his pocket.

Luke looked at the tool in Johnny's hand in astonishment. It was a pair of pliers which had wire-cutting knotches on the side. They would be able to cut through the chainlink fence.

'I thought we might come up against a fence,' smiled Johnny. 'You get to learn these things out here in the country.'

'Johnny, you're a marvel,' said Mary.

'Yes,' Tam added.

Luke said a little grudgingly, 'Well done – I wouldn't have thought of it.'

Johnny then proceeded to cut a large hole in the fence, through which they all stepped.

'I've made it big,' he said, 'in case we have to run . . .'

Luke nodded, impressed, now recognising in Johnny someone who thought things through. He was beginning to admire the country boy, despite their earlier clash.

'Right,' said Mary, organising her troops. 'Johnny and Luke can climb up the two trestles to the pipe ends, one each side, while Billy and me hand lumps of clay to Tam. Tam then passes the clay on to you two boys, who stuff it down the pipes. It's called a chain operation. Any questions?'

'No,' said Luke, a little miffed that his earlier chieftainship had been usurped by Mary, 'I think we've got our orders.'

'Well then, let's get to it,' hissed Billy.

Luke and Johnny began to climb the trestles. In front of them the marshes were murmuring. There were crickets making their usual rasping sounds. Bullfrogs were hiccoughing in the creeks. Occasionally, one of the hundreds of birds resting in the reeds during the dark hours gave out a sharp cry of alarm as a predator stalked near to it.

It was all very exciting. Luke was beginning to

think they should have put blacking on their faces, like real saboteurs. He felt like a hero about to create some great historic change in the course of events. What he would have given to see the faces of the enemy when they tried to pump the water from the marshes!

By the time he reached the top of the trestle and could see that Johnny was also in place on the top of his perch, Tam was ready to hand them a clod of clay each. Tam was not quite tall enough to reach them, but with a short toss the clay was in their hands. Luke found he had to cling on tightly with his legs, to leave his hands free for the catch.

He jammed his first lump of clay down the pipe.

'Let's have some more, Tam,' he called softly.

'Yes, come on,' whispered Johnny.

Below them, Luke saw Tam suddenly stiffen, look around him wildly and then whisper, 'Listen – the crickets . . . they've heard somethin' the matter. Somebody's coming from the river way – coming through the marshes. Svyen don't like it, he don't. Svyen's says we got to run away.'

Luke listened.

The crickets' note had indeed changed, very subtly, and the bullfrogs had stopped their croaking. Although he was not good at recognising country noises, even Luke was aware that an intruder had disturbed the marsh creatures. He held his breath for a moment. It occurred to him that Mary, Billy and Tam could get away. He opened his mouth to tell them to scatter and run.

Then, before Luke could speak, there was the hard sound of a click somewhere in the night.

At that moment the world was full of dazzling light. Luke almost fell off his trestle, blinded as he was by the intensity of the brightness. He heard Johnny utter a sound of surprise, then came a voice thundering through a loudspeaker.

'STAY WHERE YOU ARE. THIS IS THE POLICE. DO NOT MOVE FROM WHERE YOU ARE STANDING.'

The police! They had obviously encircled them. Trembling, Luke clung to the trestle with all four limbs as dark shapes came running out of the brilliance to the foot of the trestles. Tam was grabbed by two of the shadowy figures. Mary and Billy were caught by others.

'Come down from there,' said a policeman with a flat hat, calling up to Luke and Johnny.

The two boys did as they were told.

The one in the flat hat turned out to be an

inspector. He said to Tam, 'What's this then? Fagin and his gang?'

'We're not thieves,' shouted Mary angrily. 'We're trying to save the marsh from being destroyed.'

'You hold your tongue, miss,' warned the inspector. 'And you . . .' he pointed at Tam. 'You're in a lot of trouble, squire – corrupting minors, inciting them to acts of wanton vandalism . . .'

'I've just said,' Mary interrupted again, 'it's not *wanton* destruction. It has a purpose. We're trying to save the birds. You wouldn't understand.'

'Oh, I understand all right,' said the inspector. 'I understand this man is going to be charged with several counts of breaking the law, and you children won't get away scot-free either. You've got to take responsibility for your part.'

Tam stood wide-eyed and trembling before the inspector as if he were about to be executed.

Luke said quietly, 'Leave him alone. Can't you see how scared Tam is? He's a dengie. He's not used to people at all. Don't keep shouting at him. Anyway, us kids came here of our own free will. In fact, it was me and Mary who made up the plan, not Tam. Tam's just doing what we told him to.'

Normally Luke would not have spoken to a

policeman in quite such a brazen manner, but Tam's plight gave him the courage to do so. He could see the tall man was utterly terrified and thoroughly confused by the lights and the talk. His eyes were like those of some wild geese about to be shot.

'Tam?' said the Inspector. 'Your name is Tam, I suppose?' he said, looking into Tam's face. The inspector must have seen at that point that Tam was a little different from the average man in the street. He stared at him for a few moments, then said, 'Take him away. Charge him, then let him go.'

Just at that moment a man stepped out of the lights which ringed the group. He was tall, broad-shouldered, and he wore an expensive-looking suit. On the large man's face was an expression of utter contempt, presumably intended for Luke and his friends.

'I don't think you're handling this correctly,' said the man flicking cigar ash on to the grass. 'I want that fellow put in prison.'

'Mr Pritchard,' said the inspector. 'Please be careful with that cigar. It's not difficult to start a fire amongst the grasses out here on the edge of the marsh.'

'I want him in prison,' repeated Jason Pritchard,

pointing the lit cigar at Tam. The end of the cigar flared and glowed in the night breeze, as if condemning the victim.

Tam started stuttering something about the birds, but could not get it out with any clearness.

The inspector said quietly, 'I can't put a man in jail for tossing lumps of clay down the end of drainage pipes. Let's keep a sense of proportion here, Mr Pritchard. We've found the people who are causing the trouble – now we know them, there won't be any further problems. Now kindly leave the administration of the law to *me*.'

Pritchard pointed at the inspector now. 'You just make sure you do your job. If I get any more interference from people like these, I'll go to the top. Do you get my meaning, inspector?'

The inspector started to say he did not take kindly to threats, but by that time Jason Pritchard was walking away, not paying any attention. Tam and the children were marched out of the edge of the marshes to waiting police vans. Tam was taken away in one of them, while the children were put in another.

'Right,' said a constable who had climbed in the back with them, 'names and addresses . . .' He opened a notebook.

Johnny was dropped off at his house with a sergeant, while the inspector went on to Joe and Cynthia's house.

Joe came to the door. 'Who is it?' he called.

'The police, Mr Jackson.'

The children heard the bolt on the front door being drawn. Joe stood in the doorway in his pyjamas, staring out at them. His face registered utter astonishment. 'Mary? Billy? Luke? What's going on . . .?'

'If I could just step inside, Mr Jackson?' said the inspector.

Half an hour later, Joe was shaking his head.

'I can't believe it. You three ought to be ashamed of yourselves . . .' Cynthia was sitting tight-lipped in her old dressing-gown after having made a cup of tea for the inspector and his constable. So far she had only listened. Joe continued, 'I don't know what to do with you. I suppose it was you who smashed them pipes other day?'

'It was me,' Luke said. 'Mary and Billy didn't come with me that time.'

'Well, you're going to have to apologise to Mr Pritchard then, Luke. It's probably caused him a lot of trouble.'

Cynthia interrupted her husband.

'Joe, you and me – well, we kind of agree with the kids about all this, so don't you go giving the inspector the idea that we approve of what's happenin' to our marsh. The children shouldn't have done what they did, but it seems to me no great harm's been done. We'll pay for the pipes that was smashed by Luke the other day – will that put an end to it, inspector?'

The inspector looked a little put out. 'Well, there's a question of punishment.'

'You don't expect us to beat them, do you?' said Cynthia.

'No – no, not that. But they ought to be made aware that destroying other people's property – even if we, that is, they don't approve of what that property is being used for – well, that sort of thing can't be encouraged, you know.'

'They'll be made to understand that,' said Cynthia. 'Luke will have to go back to his mum . . .'

Luke suddenly realised that he was in a weak position. He had not expected this to happen. He had forgotten that his aunt and uncle had power over his movements. He didn't *want* to go away, at least until the end of the summer. He wasn't ready to say goodbye to the marshes, just when he had come to know them. The birds and other creatures needed him. It was still important to save the marshes from the march of concrete.

'NO!' he cried and rushed from the room, into the kitchen, and out through the back door which he had left unlocked earlier in the evening. There were shouts behind him, but Luke kept on running along the track to the dyke. Once on the river wall he raced along its high, snaking path, not daring to look behind him in case he was being chased. In fact, he had left the adults standing, having caught them by surprise. He had escaped and got clean away.

The tide was on the ebb now and the familiar smell of rotting shellfish and mud attacked his nose when he stopped to take deep breaths. When he had left the house he had no plan in his head, but one was beginning to form there now. He decided to go to Tam's houseboat and stay there until Tam returned. Mary and Johnny knew where it was but they would surely keep the location a secret. Luke knew he would be safe there for a while. Certainly the police would not find him without help. The salt marsh was a maze of deep creeks at that point and unless they used a helicopter, they would never locate the wreck. Besides, there were *many* wrecks in the creeks. They would have to search them all, one by one, until they found him.

When he reached the marine ply house on the deck of the old hulk, Tam was not there. No doubt, thought Luke, they're still questioning him down at the police station. Luke worried that Tam would be tongue-tied and unable to defend himself.

Luke made himself comfortable. He was exhausted by the night's events, physically, mentally and emotionally. The barge had now settled down on the mud again, in a slightly different position and at a new angle. The flood had done little damage to the cabin itself, though the deck was still damp. Luke arranged some of the orange boxes into a raised bed and immediately fell asleep on top of them.

When Luke woke it was morning. The sun was sparkling on the swinging lamp in the doorway of the cabin and a lanyard was slapping the mast almost rhythmically. There was a fresh breeze blowing through the craft, drying out its timbers.

Luke stared out into the blinding light. The sun was low on the horizon. There was a shining haze round the bows of the houseboat, where the sunlight struck first the water, then the rays glanced up again and flooded the area with brilliance. Narrowing his eyes, Luke thought he could see a silhouette inside the aura of radiant light: the shape of a broad-shouldered man. As he peered, screwing up his eyes against the brightness, it seemed as though the figure . . . saluted him.

But, then it was gone, like moisture from the marsh air under the morning sun, like vapours winding from the reeds are carried away by the prevailing winds.

The birds of the marshes and river were now awakening, unaware of the night's drama on their behalf. They called to one another down the reaches of the creeks, establishing their territories, informing their mates of the best feeding grounds. From his position on the boxes, Luke could see an oyster-catcher through the open doorway, dipping its beak into the mud, probing, shovelling, stabbing.

Breakfast! Watching the birds eat made Luke feel hungry. He searched the cabin for food and found a tin of evaporated milk.

A further search revealed a steel marline-spike, which he used to pierce two holes in the can. He drank down half the milk, then felt a little sick and dreadfully thirsty. He knew where Tam's rainwater cache was kept and helped himself to a long draught of cool water.

While he was sitting there, wondering what to do next, Tam arrived looking distressed. The tall man said nothing to Luke at first, but grabbed a long pointed stave from the corner of the cabin. Luke watched him go out on to the mud and wade slowly and carefully along a ray of water which was curling round the creek. Then came a moment when Tam seemed to freeze in the morning light, in the way that a heron poises motionless before the kill. A second later the spear flashed down. It came up with a wriggling flatfish, a dab, securely pierced.

Tam brought the fish back to the craft and cooked it over his little primus stove, giving Luke half. Once he had some food inside him, Tam obviously felt better able to speak. He turned sorrowful eyes on Luke.

'Svyen didn't like that place, much,' said Tam. 'They keeped on talking and talking and talking. Lots of people out there. Lots and lots.'

Luke's skin tingled with alarm. Of course, they would be out searching for *him*.

'Did they follow you, Tam?'

'They try to,' said Tam with satisfaction in his tone, 'but me and Svyen, we didn't let 'em.'

No one knew the marshes better than a dengie like Tam, and Luke had no doubt the men had lost his trackers. He could move at speed through the boggy swamp, while others had to pick their way carefully, watching where they trod. Tam would have come over the marsh like a deer in flight, while his pursuers plodded painfully behind. Still, there was a chance they had seen the direction and general area where Tam was heading, and Luke knew they would scour the landscape for him.

Tam said mournfully, 'They got them bulldozer machines out there – long line of 'em. I think they's going to fill in the creeks with 'em, see. Svyen don't like them bulldozers.'

It was mid-morning. The draining of the marsh would soon be underway. If Tam had seen the bulldozers lining up, it meant that Pritchard's men were going to simultaneously drain and fill the creeks as they moved across the marsh. The destruction was soon to begin and, short of throwing themselves in front of the bulldozers, there was nothing Luke and Tam could do to stop it.

It seemed the cause of the marshland birds was already lost. It was then that Luke heard the distant barking.

'Dogs!' he cried, jumping up. 'They're using dogs to track me down!'

10 A Viking funeral

'Quick!' cried Luke. 'You've got to help me, Tam. If they catch me, they're going to send me away.'

It was not that Luke wanted to remain *forever* on the marshes, or that he disliked living in the city, but he did not want to go *now*, this minute, and he had some thoughts of being a dengie like Tam for a while. He fancied catching his breakfast with a hook and line or a spear. He had ideas about becoming an expert on the wildlife of the region. He saw himself making dampers and twist over a campfire while the sun went down, big and red, into the western creeks. The winters he knew might be cruel, with freezing winds coming from the east, but in his imagination he was wrapped warmly in wild animal pelts.

Luke had forgotten for the moment that there

would shortly be no marshes, at least, not around Paglesham.

He rushed out of the cabin and over the gang-plank, not waiting to see if Tam was behind him. Not really knowing where he was going, or for what reason, Luke began to tread the hidden path to the dyke. Tam followed, but cried, 'Not that way – come this way. Follow Svyen . . .'

Luke did as he was told, turning eastwards into the heart of the marshes. Tam picked his way across the mudlands, knowing the secret ways into the tall reeds. The dogs were baying loudly now. The sound of whistles rent the air. The dogs appeared to be near. They seemed to be closing in.

Luke struggled for breath as he trod in the foot-prints of the fleet and agile Tam.

'This way,' called Tam. 'Come, come.'

A gunshot blast of knot birds exploded from the grasses just in front of Luke and frightened the wits out of him. They went up into the big bowl of the sky, wheeling and turning in unison, their under-sides flashing in the sunlight. Then came a droning sound from behind, and Luke swivelled and looked up just as a helicopter swept overhead with a rush of noise and wind which battered down the slender reeds.

'They've seen us!' cried Luke breathlessly.

More birds went up as the helicopter curved upwards away from the ground, stints and shanks this time, with a peppering of sandpipers amongst them. They flapped away in confusion, some caught in the down-draught from the rotor blades which sent them hurtling sideways on wild air currents. Tam looked at the aircraft in anguish and shook his fist at it.

'Scaring the birds!' he shrieked. 'Stop it!'

A heron took to the air, gracefully, and climbed skywards on a thermal, mimicking the circling helicopter.

The sound of barking dogs mingled with the fading noise of the helicopter as it climbed away, its job done now that it had found the runaway. Blue uniforms could be seen now, along the dyke in front of Luke and Tam. The routes out of the area into which Tam had led Luke were rapidly being closed off. The pair could stay where they were and allow the police to find their way slowly between the muddy creeks, or they could give themselves up. Luke halted, his hands on his hips, frustrated by the hopelessness of his situation.

'It's no good, Tam. They've got me. I'll have to go back to Stratford now.' Now that he was calm and thinking straight, he added, 'I don't care. I don't want to stay here and see the marshes turned into concrete.'

Tam put a hand on his shoulder in agreement. 'We can't run no more. Svyen says we've run too much now . . .'

The pair sat down on a raised knoll. Luke sighed heavily, staring around him at the lip of the creek. The police and their dogs gradually closed in. This particular creek seemed familiar to Luke, but then, he thought, they all looked much the same, the creeks. It was as if a giant had scooped out huge long troughs to which the river had later cut channels and filled with brackish water and mud. Then the wildlife had settled in and around these tidal basins.

Something unusual caught his eye and made him stand up again quickly. His eyes opened wide.

A rush of energy surged through him and he wanted to jump and shout, dance and sing, all at once; yet he could do nothing but stare, hardly daring to believe what lay before his eyes. It was as if the earth had given him the greatest prize it had to offer. There, below him, faintly outlined in the slick mire, was the longboat shape he had seen when he had first entered the marshes.

127

It was the Viking ship: the longboat of the Norse warriors who had raided the marshes a thousand years ago. Some of the mud had been washed clean away and Luke could now see the wonderful dragonhead prow. It was pitted and scarred, but the shape of the dragon was still there.

Luke suddenly realised what had happened and why the Danish ship had disappeared when he had brought his uncle out to see it. When the tide went in and out, it left humps and gouges in the creeks, but not always in the same places. The tide rushed in through the channels, scoured away mud from one part and deposited it in another. It was covering and uncovering objects all the time: old jetty posts, oyster corrals, wrecks, sunken buoys, concrete mooring blocks, all the debris of the river-bed.

The recent very high tide had obviously changed the shape of the marsh landscape and, in doing so, had once more revealed the old ship which the preserving mud had kept whole over the many centuries since the marsh raiders had left.

Tam, seeing the shape too, said, 'That's Svyen's ship, that is. He was drowned away in that ship.'

'Yes!' cried Luke, punching the air. 'Yes! Yes!'

The police inspector was the first to arrive on the knoll and he shook his head at Luke.

'You led us a fine dance, young man. Your aunt and uncle were very worried about you – and your mother. She's here now, waiting at the house. I think you'd better come along . . .'

Luke pointed triumphantly towards the hulk in the mud.

'You've got to stop the bulldozers, sir. That's a Viking ship, that is. It's – it's an antique.'

The inspector frowned, looking down into the mud. By now, some of his men had caught up with him, holding back the Alsatian dogs which were straining at their leashes. Everyone looked hot and bothered, and glared at Luke and Tam.

'Are you sure?'

'Viking people,' said Tam, nodding his head hard. 'Norsemen from the sea.'

The inspector turned to his sergeant. 'What do you think, John? You think that's a museum piece?'

'Looks like a lump of mud to me,' grunted the sergeant. 'But you know, they found that corpse – what did they call him? Pete Marsh? He was thousands of years old, buried in a peat-bog and preserved by the muck. He was older than a Viking boat anyway. Maybe we ought to play it safe and leave a man here – call someone? Could be important.'

The inspector said, 'Well, I wouldn't want to

make a mistake. We'll do as you say. Now, come on you – let's get you back to your family.'

Luke heaved a sigh of relief and followed the inspector out of the marsh and on to the dyke.

Luke's mother was beside herself when he arrived at the house. His aunt and uncle were also upset. When Luke tried to tell them he might have saved the marshes and its wildlife by finding the Viking ship, no one would listen to him. They all wanted to talk at him, tell him off, hug him, embarrass him, make him promise never to do anything like it again.

Only Mary whispered, 'Oh, Luke, let's hope this will save the birds.'

Billy grinned and said, rather more loudly, 'The Old Ben caught you then, did they, Luke?'

'Old *Bill*,' growled Luke.

'I thought it was *Big* Bill?' said his cousin.

Luke laughed, 'That's *Big Ben*. Your are a joker, Billy – I'll miss your silly games.'

Billy just grinned again.

It was only when things had calmed down that Luke was able to impress upon his mother and his relations the importance of the find he had made. They saw then that if the ship was genuine his behaviour was justified.

After a lot of pleading and promises, Luke managed to persuade his mother that he would be better off with his uncle and aunt for the rest of the summer. There were another two weeks to go. Joe and Cynthia were hesitant at first, but Luke persuaded them too.

'But you do as you're told from now on then,' said Joe. 'No more skylarking.'

'I promise,' Luke replied, meaning it.

An archaeologist arrived from the British Museum the following day and, after an examination of the sunken ship, immediately sent for a team of excavators to set up a dig. Jason Pritchard was ordered to cease work on the marina, since the marshes were now declared a site of national interest. Where there was one Viking longship, there might be more, and in any case, there were possible Norse weapons and perhaps treasure to retrieve.

Pritchard declared he had no use for land which could not be turned into a profit and sold the Paglesham marshes to the Royal Society for the Protection of Birds. Thus they were to be preserved in their present state for the foreseeable future. The old marsh raiders, the Vikings, had managed to drive out the new marsh raiders, Jason Pritchard and his men.

The excavation work was very small scale in

comparison to the marina and did very little to disturb the wildlife of The Dengies. Tam Goodson, after some twitchers wrote to the RSPB, was appointed one of the wardens of the preserve and given a small house on the edge of Paglesham Eastend.

Tam was fined by the court for his part in the pipe-smashing episode, while Luke was given a warning. They both said they were sorry to have caused so much trouble. Nothing further was said about the second incident, since the police had arrived before any serious damage could be wreaked.

The rest of the summer, Luke, Mary and Johnny helped to rebuild the hides smashed by Jason Pritchard's men. The materials were supplied by Tam's new employers, but they allowed him to design them, since he was aware of the local nesting, feeding and breeding sites of the birds. He fitted them into the contours of the marshes so well that visitors declared they could not see them until they were actually inside one. The first four hides were named Mary's Hide, Luke's Hide, Billy's Hide and Johnny's hide.

One hot day in September, Luke was lying on the deck of Tam's houseboat when he thought about the Viking warrior once more. There were just the two of them, Tam and himself, lazing away the afternoon in the warm breezes. Luke wondered whether Svyen was down at the evacuation sight, watching his longboat being uncovered, labelled and preserved by the museum people.

'You don't mention Svyen any more,' he said to Tam. 'Is he still here on the boat?'

'Of course he is,' Tam stated, tugging on a fishing line he had cast into the creek. 'He lives here don't he?'

Luke went up on his elbows.

'What do you mean "He lives here"?'

Tam shrugged his lean, brown shoulders. 'Down there,' he nodded, 'under them bows.'

Luke stared at the bows of the boat and, for the first time, noticed the hairline cracks of what appeared to be a hatch. He got up and tried to lift the trapdoor. It wouldn't budge for him. Tam, seeing what was happening, tied his line to the king post, took out his jackknife and then levered the trapdoor open so they could see into the hold.

Luke peered down into the hold, lit now by the bright noonday sun overhead. When he saw what was down there, he jumped back with a start, his heart beating rapidly.

'A skeleton,' he said hoarsely.

133

'Them's Svyen's bones. I found 'em in Brandy Creek. It's h-him all right.'

Luke went forward again and steeled himself for another look. When he got up his courage enough, he gazed down into the hold. It was more a jumble of bones and rags than a corpse, with the skull, which had made Luke jump away, sitting on top of them, looking up at the sky with eyeless sockets. The bones were stained with marsh juices to a nicotine yellow colour and were covered in cracks and fissures.

If Svyen's corpse had been preserved when Tam had hauled it from the mud, it had fallen to bits now. There was a rusty sword and a helmet lying by the bones, almost in as bad a condition as Svyen himself.

'The museum people might want those things,' said Luke. 'Maybe even Svyen too!'

Luke looked across the marshes to where a team of people were working on resurrecting the Viking ship. They had built a wall of wooden planks all round the basin in which the craft lay, as a barrier to keep out the tidal waters. Thus they could work non-stop without having to wait for the mud to be vacated by the sea. Pumps worked full-time, too, getting rid of any excess water that found its way into the hollow. Luke could hear them working, calling to each other, using winches to lift the heavier beams.

'Svyen don't want to go to no museum,' said Tam. 'He wants his funeral, he said.'

Luke blinked at Tam. 'His funeral? He wants to be buried?'

'I said that to him, but he said no he wants a *Viking* funeral – a p-p-proper one, so's he can go to Valhalla – that heaven place of his.'

'Then why don't you give him one?' asked Luke.

Tam looked at Luke with misty eyes. 'He won't tell me how,' he said helplessly. 'He can't do things like that, being a ghost. We've g-got to find out, see.'

'That's easy!' cried Luke, jumping to his feet. 'We've got to put him in a boat and set fire to it!'

Tam's eyes widened. 'Is that all?'

'Wait,' cried Luke, excited. 'We should put a sword in his hand too . . .' He looked down at the grisly remains below and shuddered a little as he thought of taking one of those bony, claw-like hands and wrapping them round the rusty sword hilt. 'You can do that if you like, Tam.'

'All right,' cried Tam, catching some of the excitement. 'I w-w-will.'

Luke ran home and fetched Mary, Billy and Johnny Elms. He told them that they were entitled to attend the Viking funeral too. Mary said she thought they ought to tell the authorities about the skeleton, but Luke reminded her that Tam had already messed about with it and would probably get into more trouble.

'They'll call him a grave-robber, or something, and accuse him of trying to hide national treasures.'

'But it's an ancient warrior.'

'Even ancient warriors are entitled to proper graves,' said Luke. 'It's disrespectful to stick them in museums for people to gawp at. Svyen wouldn't want to be laid out in a glass case for a load of school kids to jeer at, would he? And the sword and helmet are almost rusted away. They've got plenty of weapons and things in museums already.'

'You make a convincing argument,' she told Luke. 'I suppose we're doing the right thing . . .'

'That's the ticket,' cried Johnny Elms, caught up in the fervour of the moment. 'A Viking funeral!'

Tam made a small reed boat and caulked it with mud. It was not the most reliable craft in the world and was only a metre and a half long, but it would support Svyen's bones long enough for a funeral to take place. Tam was the only one who would touch the raggedy yellow bones. He placed them carefully in the reed dinghy, in more or less the right positions but with the leg bones all alongside each other, to save length.

Finally, Tam put the battered, rusty helmet on the ghastly skull and the crumbling sword in the gruesome right hand.

Luke had to admit Svyen looked quite peaceful lying there in the bottom of the reed boat, ready to pass into the hall of Odin's heroes.

As the sun went down and dark lanes of purple light appeared in thick bands over the high retreating tidal waters, the group stood on the top of a dyke above the wide muddy river. Old newspapers had been stuffed around Svyen's remains. Tam lit these with a flourish, until they were burning fiercely. Luke then pushed the reed boat out with a long stick into the slow flow of water swirling between the banks of the river.

The blazing reed boat spun slowly and lazily a couple of times when it hit eddies, but then it floated on the ebbtide, down the river towards the sea. The scene was spectacular, Luke had to admit, with the flames from the little funeral craft licking the red glow on the evening sky, gathering more scarlets and crimsons for their magnificent cause.

Black smoke drifted heavenwards, like the dark hair of a warrior being lifted by the wind.

The floating pyre went down past the workers on the evacuation site. One or two heads appeared over the flood barrier, to stare at the boat, which now crackled and sent out a smell of burning over the warm marshes. A comment was made by one of the diggers, but then someone yelled something about getting the spotlights on, since it would soon be dark. The heads disappeared again, into the dig, and Svyen was allowed to continue his journey peacefully down the river to the ocean.

Soon what remained of his last vessel was on the grey face of the North Sea, the very waters he had sailed a thousand years ago in search of Anglo-Saxon villages to ransack. He had suffered over a long time for those raids. He had been locked, imprisoned, by the land which he had pillaged so wantonly. He had now paid his dues; he was on his way to join the other Viking heroes in their world beyond death. Luke, Tam and the others, following the passage of the vessel by foot along the dyke, saw vestiges of Svyen's last small craft disappear beneath the choppy waters of the North Sea. The rituals of death had been satisfied.

'He's gone,' said Tam, sadly, already missing his constant companion. 'But he's happy now.'